Olympia knew ~~that happily-ev~~ ~~around~~ **to be a daddy just didn't happen, except in fairy tales.**

"I've dreamed about the rodeo, about leaving Arizona, since I was a little girl," she insisted...to Spence...to herself. "I've faced down plenty of reality."

"Oh, honey," he said softly as she curled into his side, her face fitting perfectly against his shoulder. Those broad, strong shoulders could stand straight against anything. "You're amazing, to have lived through all of that and come out not only a brave cowgirl but having raised your sisters, too."

"Maybe the rodeo was just a little girl's dream and now I'm a woman?"

"That you are," he said, giving her butt a squeeze.

She didn't know whether to laugh or moan, whether to be offended or excited. "Aren't you supposed to be sleeping on the floor?"

"I will." He didn't move his hand.

His kisses and soft touches caused everything to fade away. She snuggled into him.

He whispered, "What do you need, cowgirl?"

"You."

Dear Reader,

I'm back in Arizona revisiting the Leigh and MacCormack families in my second book about cowgirls and the men they love. This time attorney and father Spencer MacCormack gets tangled up with Olympia James, a footloose cowgirl from the wrong side of the trailer park. Next I mixed in a marriage of convenience, an unexpected pregnancy and a javelina (an Arizona-style pig), making *The Convenient Cowboy* just as much fun to write as my first book.

Most of my story ideas start with a scene that I see clearly in my head. For this book, it was Spence's quickie wedding in Las Vegas (or Lost Wages, as my uncle called it). His bride took longer to see, then there she was. A young woman who'd vowed that she was going to be a rodeo star and no babies or husband were going to stand in her way. Boy, did that give them a few "challenges." But no matter what I threw at them, they just couldn't stay out of each other's arms.

With the MacCormack brothers' stories told, my brain (and my fingers) have been itching to write about the other two Leigh siblings...or maybe there's another cowgirl out there who will show up in my imagination.

If you want to know more about my inspirations and musings or drop me a note, check out my website and blog at heidihormel.net, where you also can sign up for my newsletter; or connect with me at facebook.com/authorheidihormel, twitter.com/heidihormel or pinterest.com/hhormel.

Yee-haw,

Heidi Hormel

THE CONVENIENT COWBOY

HEIDI HORMEL

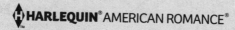
HARLEQUIN® AMERICAN ROMANCE®

If you purchased this book without a cover you should be aware that this book is stolen property. It was reported as "unsold and destroyed" to the publisher, and neither the author nor the publisher has received any payment for this "stripped book."

Recycling programs
for this product may
not exist in your area.

ISBN-13: 978-0-373-75581-3

The Convenient Cowboy

Copyright © 2015 by Heidi Hormel

All rights reserved. Except for use in any review, the reproduction or utilization of this work in whole or in part in any form by any electronic, mechanical or other means, now known or hereinafter invented, including xerography, photocopying and recording, or in any information storage or retrieval system, is forbidden without the written permission of the publisher, Harlequin Enterprises Limited, 225 Duncan Mill Road, Don Mills, Ontario M3B 3K9, Canada.

This is a work of fiction. Names, characters, places and incidents are either the product of the author's imagination or are used fictitiously, and any resemblance to actual persons, living or dead, business establishments, events or locales is entirely coincidental.

This edition published by arrangement with Harlequin Books S.A.

For questions and comments about the quality of this book, please contact us at CustomerService@Harlequin.com.

® and TM are trademarks of Harlequin Enterprises Limited or its corporate affiliates. Trademarks indicated with ® are registered in the United States Patent and Trademark Office, the Canadian Intellectual Property Office and in other countries.

Printed in U.S.A.

With stints as an innkeeper, radio talk show host and craft store manager, **Heidi Hormel** settled into her true calling as a writer. She spent years as a reporter (covering the story of the rampaging elephants Debbie and Tina) and as a PR flunky (staying calm in the face of Cookiegate) before settling into penning romances with a wink and a wiggle.

A small-town girl from a place that's been called the Snack Food Capital of the World, Heidi has trotted over a good portion of the globe, from Volcano National Park in Hawaii to Loch Ness in Scotland to the depths of Death Valley. She has also spent large chunks of time in Arizona, where she fell in love with the desert and fry bread, and in Great Britain, where she developed an unnatural obsession with jacket potatoes and toasties.

Heidi is on the web at heidihormel.net as well as socially out there at facebook.com/authorheidihormel, twitter.com/heidihormel and pinterest.com/hhormel.

Books by Heidi Hormel

Harlequin American Romance

The Surgeon and the Cowgirl

For the unflagging support of my writing friends.
It has taken a village with virtual and in-person
hand-holding to get another story
out of my brain and onto the page.
My sincerest thanks (until you're better paid).

Chapter One

"I now pronounce you man and wife. Thank you. Thank you very much," announced the standard-issue Elvis minister at the Little Chapel of the Strip in Vegas.

Not exactly how Olympia had pictured her wedding, but then she'd never planned to get married at all. So the $29.99 ceremony would do just fine.

"Thanks," her new husband, Spencer MacCormack, said as he shook Elvis's beringed hand. He used his aw-shucks-ma'am smile, which hid his sharky lawyer brain.

Olympia shook the minister's hand, too, ignoring his raised eyebrows. He was clearly wondering why they hadn't kissed. Simple answer. The marriage had been contracted, signed, sealed and delivered. No lovin'. No touchin'. No squeezin'. She'd get the cash she needed for her sister. Being a husband would get Spence full custody of his son. When they each had what they wanted, they'd go on their merry ways, just like they'd done after that night in Phoenix.

"Do you want to eat before we head back?" Spence asked as he opened the door into the desert heat, waving for her to go first. Another one of those cowboy gestures that was as fake as a three-dollar bill. She knew that Spence had grown up in suburban Phoenix—on a golf course—and had never ridden a horse and never wanted to. Even without the Stetson and drawl, his all-American good looks—the disordered blond hair, the dusty-blue eyes and the barely there dimple—probably got him what he wanted in the courtroom and in the bedroom. She blamed falling into bed with him three months ago on his looks. But that was ancient history. Over. Done.

"I just want to get back to Tucson," Olympia said. The knots in her stomach stayed firmly tied, as they had for months, ever since her youngest sister had announced that—in a stroke of James-family bad luck—her four-year college scholarship had dried up, and she'd have to drop out of school before she'd even started. When Spence had approached Olympia with the "marriage" proposal out of the blue, she'd hoped that she'd finally been cut a break.

"If traffic is good, we should be home by four," Spence said as the oversize, fuel-guzzling, dual-pipe pickup with the king cab roared to life. "If you need me to stop for a pee-pee break, just holler."

"Really? I'm not two."

"Sorry. Old habit from when I hauled my son around as a toddler." He pulled out of the parking lot.

Nausea added to her misery. When they'd been getting hitched, she'd been able to forget that Spence had a seven-year-old son who would *not* be living with them or even visiting. *Thank the Lord.* The former in-laws had his custody all tied up in court, and Spence could see his son at only neutral locations. He'd talked about that when they'd met at her friend's wedding. She'd felt bad for him. Even though they'd connected and he'd charmed her with a smile she'd found attractive at the time, she'd never imagined that they'd be involved beyond that one night. That was the kind of curveball life always threw at her, so here she and Spence were— married, with a one-hundred-page prenup contract. The document outlined a lot of how they would carry on before and after the marriage and stipulated he'd reside at her house. She'd been the one to explain that the ranch would help show he had a stable home life—no pun intended. But the overly legal agreement didn't get into the nitty-gritty of the everyday. Like, who cooked? Not her. Who cleaned the toilet? Not her.

The number one unwritten ground rule, though, had to be that she and Spence would *not* repeat what had happened in Phoenix after the wedding of Jessie, her friend, to Payson, Spence's brother. Olympia had no room in her life for romance or wannabe cowboys. She swallowed hard, bile creeping up the back of her throat, then picked up her purse and rooted for the TUMS, which had become a staple of her diet the past three weeks.

They had hours before they'd get to the foothills of the Catalina Mountains outside Tucson. She'd inherited a small ranch there from her deadbeat father. Her daddy—though she usually thought of him as The Sperm Donor—hadn't paid child support or done any of the other things a father should do. Then three years ago, he'd died and left her the ranch. Of course, the taxes hadn't been paid, the house hadn't been lived in for years and the barn, which could house only six horses, had needed major repairs. By stretching her finances beyond the breaking point, she'd made it livable...just. The ranch wasn't the only thing she'd inherited. According to Mama, Olympia looked more like her daddy with her dark hair and slanted eyes. The only thing James about her was her breasts—large and high—and her short pinkie fingers.

Get it over with, cowgirl, Olympia told herself. "We need to clear up the house rules. You know, like I don't do laundry, cook meals, make beds—"

"I get it," Spence said. "You're not June Cleaver. But let me remind you that I may need to show the courts that I have an appropriate home life, in case of an official visit."

Olympia gulped down the tension that had lodged in her throat. She plucked three lint-covered TUMS from the bottom of her bag and chewed. "As long as you're clear about me *not* being the wifely type. I'm not a slob, but I don't clean up after anyone but me." The idea of being tied down to a man made her want to howl and chew off her leg like a coyote caught in a trap. She had this one final thing to do for her youngest sister. Then her responsibility to her family was over and done with. James women looked after themselves—only—just like her mama had said again and again.

"You don't have to be anything," Spence said, his eyes never leaving the road as he raced down the highway. "You can act, can't you?"

"Act like a damned Stepford wife from the sounds of it."

"No swearing. You're the mother—stepmother—of an impressionable young boy."

"What the hell? I won't be seeing him. He's not coming to the ranch. How much can I corrupt him?" The temporary marriage would barely register for the boy. She should know. She'd had at least six "daddies." And what did she remember about any of them, even her own? Next to nothing.

"We need to be prepared for the possibility of a court examiner coming to the house. That person will expect a home where there isn't swearing or yelling, and there are snacks and sit-down meals."

The antacids hadn't touched the nausea or the burning in her stomach. "That's not what we agreed to. I've got a life, you know."

"Obviously," he said, glancing at her, "the judge will need to see a report clearly showing that, unlike my ex, I can provide a stable, loving home."

"There isn't anything in the prenup about not swearing."

"In section four, paragraph six, I included a morality clause."

"A what?"

"Morality clause. You know, no messing around with other men, no drinking—"

"Well, slap me stupid, I didn't know I'd hitched my wagon to a preacher's."

"This is my son."

She'd seen a picture of the pale, frail little boy, wearing plaid pants and a sweater vest—nerdy anywhere, but in Arizona, his clothes were a billboard that said Kick Me. "Fine. No swearing. I'll try, *if* the examiner ever comes."

"Get into the habit now."

"Whatever," she said, sticking out her chin to show him that he couldn't intimidate her. She swallowed hard. She never got carsick. Must be the air-conditioning blowing his unwelcome, but familiar, scent of leather, desert and black licorice into her face.

SPENCE GLANCED OVER, wondering where the sexy cowgirl he'd met at Payson's wedding had gone. Today she looked rode hard and put away wet. They hadn't married for keeps, but couldn't she have pretended she cared that it was her wedding? Maybe the cowgirl-hobo look was a thing? On the other hand, he didn't want to remember taking off the silky dress she'd worn to Payson's wedding, revealing the lacy bra and panties... Nope...shouldn't think about that night in her Phoenix motel room.

Sleeping together wasn't part of what they'd agreed to, no matter what had happened when they'd met. He wouldn't tell his son about the Vegas wedding or about Olympia, unless he had to. Right now, Calvin was in his former in-laws' custody. On the plus side—as if there could even be a plus side—Calvin could stay in the dark about having a stepmom. If his grandparents said anything, Spence would come up with a story that he hoped would hold up under Calvin's questioning, which had become nearly as sharp as Spence's own. It was hard not to feel proud of his son's intelligence, even while it could be a huge pain in Spence's butt.

He pushed his son to the back of his mind because he had to deal with Olympia first by making her understand the importance of the marriage. Or maybe reiterate the importance. The one-hundred-page prenuptial contract explained the details, but he had the feeling that he needed to appeal to her emotions again. When they'd talked at his brother's wedding, she'd been sympathetic. She'd hinted that her own childhood had been less than ideal, but she'd spoken of her youngest sister with a lot of affection and pride, telling him how the girl had gotten a full-ride scholarship, which had disappeared just a month later. Clearly, at times, her family exasperated her, but she loved them and felt responsible for their welfare. So when he'd come up with the crazy idea of a marriage to gain custody of Calvin, she'd immediately sprung to mind. He figured that she'd agree to all this for her sister. No matter what she said now about not wanting to meet Calvin or get too involved, she understood sacrifice and love for family.

Spence looked at the passing sign. Hours to her ranch, where they'd live—a negotiating point she'd refused to give on. His brother, Payson, would have a good laugh at Spence living on a working ranch, not a prettily landscaped one like those their friends' families had owned when they were growing up. Spence wore the trappings of a cowboy and drove an oversize truck because it was what his clients expected. Everyone assumed a native Arizonan like him was a cowboy, but he was a city boy through and through.

He pulled in a deep breath, catching her oddly erotic scent of Granny Smith apples and smoky chipotle, before he put on his lawyer face. "You've laid out your expectations, but there are some points that will need further discussion. When we met, it was clear to me that you were committed to your family, your sisters. And I believe when I 'proposed' you said, 'I'll do anything to help my sister and keep my ranch afloat.'" Sounding like such a jerk might be the reason for all the lawyer jokes. On the other hand, he'd do whatever he had to do to keep his son.

"I did not say that."

"It was implied." He glanced over and saw her tabby cat–brown eyes narrow. She pushed back a strand of dark hair that had fallen from her stubby ponytail. Did she cut her hair herself?

"I married you. That doesn't automatically make me—"

"I don't make this request without reason, and it could easily be covered under the contingency clause in section ten, subsection D."

"I don't like the sound of *contingency clause*."

"I told you to have an attorney look over the document."

"As if I have the money for that. The whole reason I even signed the da...darned thing was for the money."

"You did sign it, and there is a contingency clause." Spence changed lanes and floored the truck, hoping to outrace this sinking feeling. He'd known that the marriage, the prenup contract and moving to the ranch had been desperation on his part... Hers, too. It wasn't just the marriage that he needed. He hadn't really made that clear during the negotiations. A lawyer tactic. He hadn't lied, but she hadn't asked, so... "As I said, we may have to submit to the court sending someone into our home to determine its suitability. My lawyer and I are also fighting for Calvin to have a chance to visit me while we negotiate for custody—"

"Excuse me, but that was *not* in the agreement or in anything we discussed."

"The contingency clause—"

"My a—" He glared at her. "Aunt Fanny. You told me that Calvin didn't live with you. That was the whole reason for the wedding."

"Right. To get custody of my son. Didn't you ever hear that possession is nine-tenths of the law, darlin'?"

She clamped her mouth closed, barely moving her

lips when she said, "I married you for the money. You said this wouldn't be a real marriage. I'm holding you to that, lawyer boy."

He tightened his hands on the wheel and glared hard at the white SUV in front of them to stop himself from blurting out something he'd have to apologize for later. Why was he so annoyed that she didn't want to be near his child? That was what he wanted. He didn't want Calvin to think of her as a new mommy.

"If," he emphasized, "I'm granted a visit, maybe you could go stay with your family. You and he wouldn't need to meet." Had he overplayed his hand? He glanced sideways to gauge her annoyance, noticing the sharpness of her jaw. Had she lost weight? What words was she holding back? How the hell had things gotten so complicated? For maybe the first time in his life, he decided to keep his mouth shut.

"I told you I don't have the mothering gene." She sucked in a breath, her face paling. "It is *my* ranch, so why do I have to leave?"

The way she talked about her sister, he was pretty sure she did have a mothering gene. But that didn't matter now, because he was stuck. He'd let the lease go on his apartment—his crappy apartment—and he wouldn't have the funds to pay for her sister's tuition and the apartment anyway. He also had to pay his attorney. Spence had represented himself before, and it'd been a disaster. The case was too emotional. His attorney had let him slide on his bills before, but that had come to an end last month.

He knew how to negotiate. He'd drop the argument, change the subject and let her think that she'd won for now, then come back later and work on her. "I got us a room at the Ritz-Carlton at Dove Mountain, outside Tucson. The honeymoon suite."

"Excuse me?" she asked in a tone that suggested that she wanted to eviscerate him.

"I don't want anyone to think this marriage isn't real. They might understand that we can't immediately go on a big honeymoon, but we have to take at least one night. I'll have the receipts."

"Great. You can stay at the hotel. I've got animals to see to."

"Someone is going out to the ranch to care for the stock tonight, too."

"You have a stranger at my place, without my permission?"

"It's my ranch, too."

She made a sound that could have come from an arched-backed, bushy-tailed cat. Once again, his mouth had worked faster than his brain.

"Do you want me to divorce you before this farce starts? I can do it. Nonconsummation."

Any other woman would have been thrilled that he'd taken care of everything. "I apologize," he said, with little feeling. He felt her glare. "Even you have to admit that it'd look weird if we didn't have one night to celebrate. We told everybody that we were so in love that we done run off and got married." He could feel her anger, her annoyance... He wasn't sure what. Being the good ol' boy usually relaxed his clients.

"Cut the crap. You're not a cowboy." She paused for a moment, and with a smoother tone asked, "You really think someone is going to ask for receipts?"

"My ex's lawyers will. I would, if she was my client."

She snorted. "Convenient that you know what a lawyer would do."

"The reservations are made."

"You got two beds, right?"

Obviously, she saw the logic of his argument. "I doubt it. It's the honeymoon suite, but I'll sleep on the couch."

"Damn right, you will," she said. "We've got to stop at the ranch, no matter what. I don't have anything with me for an overnight stay."

"There's a bag in the back—"

"You went through my stuff?" she said, her voice rising.

"I stopped at the drugstore and picked up what I thought you'd need. You'd be amazed what they have."

He glanced over and noted her stiff posture, along with the small frown line between her dark brows that made the tilt of her eyes even more catlike.

"You can order anything you like from room service," he wheedled, using the voice that he'd perfected while married to Missy, the one that calmed cranky women. He resented having to placate her, but that was where he was if he wanted this balancing act to net him custody of his son.

"Don't patronize me," she snapped. "I will do this tonight because it'll make this marriage—" she spit out the word "—appear real. You pull crap like this again, and I'll invoke the you-need-me-as-much-as-I-need-you clause." She stared at him hard before she went on, "I'm an adult woman and expect to be consulted when you make decisions. This is not a dictatorship. I might not have a degree or a fancy address, but I know when I'm being played."

"Duly noted," he said, his grip relaxing just a fraction. How was he going to get through this marriage? The same way he'd made it through the first four years of Calvin's life, protecting him from his increasingly addicted mother—one day at a time and using every trick he'd learned in the courtroom.

"Also, make a note to yourself to stay out of my personal life."

"It won't be so bad, darlin'." He tried his hearty, cajoling voice again. "You know there are people who think I'm plumb charmin'."

"Yeah, well, people said the same thing about Hannibal Lecter."

Her last words came out as a gulping sound, the kind Calvin made just before he hurled. He turned to her. "You okay?"

"It's your crappy cologne. It's enough to make anyone want to toss her cookies."

"Did you eat anything today? Maybe we should stop."

"Pull over."

"I didn't mean now."

"Pull over, or I'm puking all over your pretty truck. Right now." She swallowed again, and he saw the sheen of sweat on her forehead. He swerved to the far right, ignoring the horns, skidding onto the gravel. Olympia pushed open the door before the truck came to a full stop and vomited into the dust at the side of the road.

He got out and raced to her. It might not be a real marriage, but she was a human being. She dry heaved for a moment and moaned in misery. He pulled open the door to the king cab and rooted for a bottle of water.

"Drink this."

"I'll just throw up again."

"Rinse out your mouth." He didn't let her refuse. She took a long swig and handed him the bottle. He went back into the cab for paper towels, wet one and put it on her neck. "Do you think it's the flu or something?"

She shook her head and leaned over, eyes squeezed shut. "It must have been something I ate."

"You didn't eat anything this morning."

"That's probably it." She sucked in a breath. "I'm so dizzy. This is the fourth day in a row."

"Fourth day?" Spence asked, his quick lawyer's mind putting together the facts into a new pattern.

"Yeah," she said, pursing her lips as a breath gusted out.

"Oh, Christ." He sagged a little against the door. No. No way. "When was your last period?"

"None of your damned business," she said and then leaned over again, although there was nothing left in her stomach.

He had to be wrong. It was the flu. It was the dreaded Hantavirus. It was… Dear Lord, three months ago in a Phoenix motel room, there'd been that broken condom.

"Olympia," he started, cleared his throat and tried again before all his words dried up. "Could you be pregnant?"

Chapter Two

Olympia's hand shook as she tried to pee on the stick for the superfast pregnancy results, which had to be negative. She could not be pregnant. She would not be pregnant. She had plans that didn't include kids, because babies led to living in a trailer hand-to-mouth like her mama and grammy. She'd worked hard to make sure she and her sisters wouldn't end up there, too. Agreeing to the proposal had gotten her youngest sister, Rickie, set for college. That meant that it was Olympia's turn to do what she wanted without worrying about someone else first...like a baby. How many more seconds? Too many.

She wanted to throw up again. Her stomach flipped just below her breastbone. That couldn't be morning sickness because it had passed noon hours ago.

"It's been ten minutes," Spence said through the door. He'd almost carried her to the honeymoon suite after a quick stop at the drugstore. She'd made him go in and buy the stupid test that would prove she wasn't pregnant. She had her life mapped out. She'd go on the road with the rodeo, working with stock until she had enough money for the kind of horse that could be a star barrel racer, unlike the two horses at her ranch—rescues no one else wanted.

She didn't answer Spence. What a coward she was. Not very cowgirl of her. *Pony up and read the damned stick.*

Spence said louder, "What's going on? Did you pass out?"

"I… It's a few more minutes."

"I told you to drink more."

She wanted to moan in embarrassment and frustration. Not normally squeamish or girlie, talking with a near stranger about her bodily functions made her want to squirm. "Drinking a bunch of water after puking is not a good idea."

"I told you that I'd get you ginger ale."

She didn't think the ginger ale would stay down any better. "Go stand somewhere else."

"When Missy was pregnant with Calvin, she was only sick until the end of her fourth month, then she was fine."

"I'm not pregnant."

"The condom broke, Olympia."

"So? Do you know what the chances are of getting pregnant?"

"Really good when the condom breaks."

Didn't he get it? Being pregnant would be a disaster. James women were born without maternal instinct but with a knack for picking men who made even worse fathers. Olympia, named for the beer her mother blamed her conception on—as if any kid wanted that kind of detail about their making—had barely known her father. The only good thing he'd done for her had been leaving her the ranch. Broken-down and not much more than scrub and sand, but it was still hers—if she could deal with the back taxes, the current taxes and all the other bills.

Like her mama, who she'd vowed she'd never be like, Olympia now stood in a bathroom, waiting to find out if another James baby was on the way, this one to a pretend cowboy with a kid and a crazy ex. The kind of country-and-western song she didn't want her life to be. Olympia's eyes burned with tears. She wanted to sob and wail, but she couldn't do any of that because she had to hold it together. A stranger stood on the other side of that door. A man she'd met at a friend's wedding and who should have been a pleasant memory. Maybe when she was ninety and needed help getting things from the high shelf, she'd want to be tied down to a man. Until then, she'd follow the rodeo.

"It's way past time."

Olympia started, and the stick skittered across the bathroom tile.

"You okay?"

She crawled on the floor. The doorknob rattled. Her head swam. She stopped all movement, not sure whether she was going to pass out, throw up or just die of fear.

"Olympia, open the damned door."

A giggle burst from her, the sound echoing in the gigantic bathroom, which would fit two of her bathrooms at the ranch.

"I'm going to break down the door if you don't stop laughing."

"Drama queen…wait…guess that's drama king." Her hysterical giggles escalated. The door handle jiggled violently. She sat against the vanity, ignoring the stick half a bathroom away. If she didn't look, then it would go away. Even as that thought flashed through her head, she knew it was infantile, but her brain just wouldn't accept that she could be pregnant. Not after all her vows and precautions and all the times she'd told her mama that she'd never have kids.

Thud. "Damn," muttered Spence. He really was going to break down the door. Afraid to stand on her noodly legs, Olympia crawled to the door, then just stared at the handle as it forcefully shook.

"Open the door, Olympia," Spence said in a new voice, neither authoritative nor wheedling. "We'll take care of this."

He said that now, but… She reached up and unlocked the door, catching a glimpse of the stick. In that moment her whole life passed before her eyes. Who was the drama queen now? She scooted away and sat again with her back pressed into the vanity, her head on her knees, gulping down the nausea and dizziness. Was this how Mama had felt the first time she'd gotten pregnant? Sick, scared and, crazily enough, hungry for animal crackers with hot sauce? Olympia stifled another moan of misery and embarrassment.

SPENCE OPENED THE door slowly, not sure what he'd find in the bathroom. He hadn't heard anything that sounded like Olympia tearing up the room, but his ex-wife, Missy, had taught him destruction could take place in complete silence.

"Did you look?" he asked softly, kneeling beside her. She gulped hard. He didn't move, trying to decide what the sound meant, then he saw the stick on the floor beyond her. Three feet away. He could reach out and touch it. Not that he really needed to see it. He knew. He heard a mouse-quiet "No, no, no" coming from Olympia. He stood, took a breath and reached for the stick. Pregnant. Written as clear as day, as clear as the type on their prenuptial contract. Olympia was going to have his baby.

The caveman part of his brain did a fist pump. This woman was carrying his baby. Wait. They'd been together one night. Who knew what had happened in the months since then? He remembered again the broken condom, and his sister-in-law, Jessie, telling him that she'd been surprised to see Olympia and him paired up. Jessie'd told him how her friend was nearly a nun, usually too busy with siblings and scraping together money. That didn't mean that Olympia hadn't done the two-step with another cowboy, though.

"Olympia," he said, laying his hand gently on her back, like he would Calvin after a bad dream. "It's positive."

She shook her head.

"Now, I've got to ask. Is the baby mine?"

He never saw the punch that came at him sideways and smacked into his throat.

"I'm not a slut," Olympia said low and fiercely.

He swallowed hard around the pain. "It's a reasonable question. I only met you at the wedding, and you slept with me."

Her head snapped up from where she'd let it drop onto her knees. Her slanted eyes narrowed further, the tabby-brown darkening to near black. "So I'm the slut, and you're what, just a stud? How do I know you're not a serial impregnator? You said the broken condom was an accident, but was it?"

"'Serial impregnator'? That doesn't even make sense."

"Maybe you get some kind of sick thrill out of being

a baby daddy and abandoning your children. Men are like that."

Now she was starting to piss him off. "I have one child. I guess now I'll have two. That's it. And the reason I'm with you is because I want custody of my son."

"Probably for the child support," she muttered.

Hostile witness. Think of her as a hostile witness. He took a deep mental breath and worked on moving his features into a friendly smile, something that crossed good old boy with beta male. "Come on, darlin', the floor in here is cold, and we've got some heavy-duty jawin' to do. Let's go sit on the couch so we can figure all this out."

She pulled away from the fingers he'd laid on her shoulder. "That really works on people?" She clasped her hands together until her knuckles went white. "The test could be wrong. It says so in the fine print…"

"Darlin'—"

"Don't call me that. I am not your darlin', and you are *not* a cowpoke or whatever the hell you're pretending to be." Her chin came up, matching the flat annoyance in her eyes.

New tactic. He dropped the drawl and went for reasonable attorney. "Do you really think you're not pregnant? You've been throwing up. You haven't had your period, right? And the condom broke. How likely is it that the test is wrong?"

"It's possible."

"Take another one," he said, holding on to his reasonable tone by the last thread of his patience. "I got three different ones."

He hesitated a moment, then moved out of the bathroom to give her time for the news to sink in. He needed a few minutes, too. As an attorney, he knew how to look calm, cool and collected, even when he wasn't. He went to the bucket with its celebratory bottle of champagne. No. He hated the stuff, plus this called for something stronger. Cracking open the minibar, he got out the two tiny bottles of whiskey and gulped down the liquor in the first one without bothering to find a glass. He enjoyed the warmth as it hit his stomach and spread out from there, thawing the cold ball of dread…and excitement…that had lodged in his gut. For the second bottle, he found a glass and left the room quietly for ice.

"Oh, my God," he said to himself as he walked the corridor. A wife and a baby. That had not been how he'd imagined this day ending. Actually, his hope had been to convince her that there was no reason they shouldn't enjoy each other again. They were married, after all, and had proved that night they were compatible sexually—more than once. *The* night, apparently. He stopped in the middle of the hall with the ice bucket, trying to take in the fact that he was going to be a father again. Maybe a little girl this time?

When he got back to their room, she'd closed the bathroom door again. He poured his whiskey on the rocks, went to the window and stared out over the golf course below them. Lifting his glass to take a drink, he stopped when he saw his reflection in the window, a silly grin splitting his face. Maybe this wasn't exactly how he'd wanted things to go, but having another child, making a family would never be a bad thing.

They needed dinner—an amazing dinner with a spectacular dessert to celebrate. It was their honeymoon, and they were going to have a baby.

"Olympia, I'm ordering room service. Steak, beans,

salad, with something decadent and chocolate for dessert. Is there anything you want?" He stepped back surprised when the door opened.

"That'll be fine," she said.

He looked her over. Other than the pale face, she appeared composed, her usual competent, cowgirl self. Actually, she looked better than when they'd said, "I do" this morning. Had it only been this morning? He waited for her to say more, but she just walked past him and sat on the couch. He called in the order and worked hard to wipe the stupid, sappy grin off his face before sitting down with Olympia. She'd turned on the TV, putting it on mute.

"The food should be here in fifteen, twenty minutes." He paused, letting his brain sort through possible ways to get them on better footing. "You know Jessie from some rodeo camp you went to as kids, right?"

Olympia nodded, her eyes not meeting his. "Is there something to drink?"

"I can go to the soda machine. What would you like?"

She sat for a moment, her face blank. Then she shook herself and said, "An orange soda?"

"Sure thing. If room service comes, just put it on the room tab." He pulled his wallet from his pocket and gave her a twenty. "Here's a tip, too."

He hurried from the room. Olympia's blank eyes were disturbing. He needed to remember that she'd never gone through this before—the delight and fear of pregnancy.

HE SMELLED THE FOOD as soon as he stepped back into the room with four cans of soda, none of them orange.

He'd even tried different floors, hoping that the machines had different offerings. But no orange, so he'd gotten a variety that excluded caffeine—not good for the baby, not that any of the other ingredients were exactly healthy.

The room-service table sat by the window, covered with silver-lidded dishes. Olympia stood by it, looking out at the peaceful desert, just as he'd done.

"Why don't we eat? You'll feel better. It'll help with the nausea," he said. Her shoulders went up around her ears. "Come on. I know you're hungry. I'm starved. Plus we need to celebrate."

"Celebrate?" she whirled around, her mouth contorted in rage, pain or maybe terror.

"Sure. A baby and a wedding."

"A fake wedding and a baby that neither of us wants."

"Well, at least you're admitting you're pregnant."

She barked out a laugh. "Three pee sticks don't lie. I'm a James. Of course I'm pregnant. It's what we do. Hook up with some random guy, get pregnant, hope that it'll last, then when it doesn't, look for the next guy willing to—"

"Whoa. Hold on. I won't abandon—"

"You're all puffed up and proud because your swimmers won, but it doesn't last. It never lasts." Her words devolved into a sob.

Spence took one small, slow step closer, wanting to comfort and reassure her. He picked up her hand and held it. She didn't pull back. "I'm fighting for custody of my son. I won't walk away from another child." His heart flopped again as he thought about another baby in his life.

"No," she said, pulling away. "You're not going to negotiate or talk me into this."

"I'm not talking you into anything."

"I know we're married, but it's fake. We're not a forever kind of thing."

"Maybe, but—"

She cut him off again. Her face lightened two shades, and her mouth clamped into a firm line. "I'm giving the baby up for adoption."

"What? This is my child. You can't do that."

"No. It's mine."

"I don't think so."

"Who's the one who's pregnant? Huh? Plus, we'll be divorced before I have the baby." Her chin thrust out again.

"Whether we're divorced or not, the baby is mine, too, just like Calvin. A real man doesn't walk out on his family. My God, the whole reason we're married is because I want my son in my life. Why do you think this baby will be any different? You can't give the baby up for adoption without my consent."

"What if I run away? I bet they wouldn't care in Mexico."

His hands went clammy, and the collar on his shirt suddenly felt too tight. Would she really do that? Or was it just fear talking? He stared at her hard, assessing her as he would an opponent across the negotiating table. Her lips trembled just a little. She wasn't an opponent. She was the mother of his baby and, for now, his wife. "You're not runnin' away, darlin'. We'll work this out," he said in his most reasonable voice.

"You can't stop me."

"That's where you're wrong. We have a contract,

and I know the law." He let that hang there because she was right. He couldn't force her to have the baby or to stay in Arizona, but by the time she figured out all that, he'd have her sign an addendum to their contract. He waited for her to say something. He hated to lie to her, but this was about his baby. He'd do whatever it took to save his child.

Chapter Three

Olympia sat down suddenly. Her head whirled; the room wavered. She couldn't think about keeping a baby, even if he told her he'd stick around. A big lump settled midway up her throat. Throw up or pass out—those were her options. Her vision started to darken around the edges. She swallowed hard.

"For God's sake," Spence said, firmly grasping her by the neck and pushing down her head.

She tried to suck in a deep breath, but her insides were being crushed. Was that what happened? She remembered Mama waddling around, pregnant with her sister Rickie. She couldn't train for the rodeo while she was pregnant, could she? What would she do? She'd waited so long to get on the circuit. "Oh, God, oh, God, oh, God," she moaned. A garbage can appeared under her nose. She batted at it. She wasn't going to be sick, and the dark spots were disappearing. She sat up and stopped moving abruptly when the room whirled again.

"Here," Spence said, thrusting a doughy white roll at her. "You said that you haven't had any food, and even if you did, you left it out there along the 10."

She cautiously took the roll. Regardless of her state of knocked-up-ness, not eating would make anyone sick.

She nibbled at the bread while he lifted the silver covers from the plates and put them back. After a deep breath, he smiled at her. She guessed it was the smile he used in court to win over the ladies on the jury.

"Looks good," he said, his dimple deepening.

She continued to munch on the bread, which seemed to settle just fine. Spence didn't sit down but watched her as though he'd taken up guard duty.

"Aren't you hungry?" she asked after finishing the roll and thinking that the steak and cowboy beans—even cooled—smelled good.

He gave her another for-the-jury smile. "No, ma'am. Not right now. Maybe later."

Great. He was back to pretending he was a cowboy. Annoyance flooded her, and bile threatened to choke her. The food was no longer tempting. "So you have me trapped in this room. What are we going to do?" she asked, not caring that she sounded belligerent.

"Well," he drawled, "I'm going to finish my drink here, then mosey on down to the bar."

"I thought you were proving to anyone who cared that we'd actually gone on a honeymoon."

"The receipts will be enough. There isn't a PI tracking us."

"Whatever." She lifted the cover on the food again, just to give her something to do, because she was not going to eat it. Maybe a milk shake would be okay. She'd call room service once he left.

"I'll see you later. Make sure you lock the door. I have my key. By the way, I'm sure I can see the lobby from the bar," Spence said.

She heard the implied threat. Still, after he'd gone, she almost missed his hint of licorice and leather. For the first time since Spence had pulled off the road for her to be sick, Olympia took a deep breath. She pushed the cart away. After calling for a triple-thick vanilla shake, she went to look through the bag of things he'd bought for their overnight stay. Thank goodness there was a T-shirt and sweatpants. At least she wouldn't have to sleep in her clothes.

She got as comfy as she could while ignoring the reality of her situation. She turned on the TV, loud, and forced herself to enjoy her extralarge milk shake.

"WHY ARE YOU sleeping here?" Spence asked later, appearing over her nest of pillows on the couch.

"This is more comfortable." The king-size bed in the other room intimidated her.

"This is where I'm sleeping. I'm not going to let a pregnant woman sleep on a couch when there's a perfectly good bed."

Fully awake now, she felt her gorge rising again at the word *pregnant*. Why had he said that? She swallowed.

"Are you going to be sick?"

"No." She shook her head but stopped quickly. Maybe the overly rich shake hadn't been such a good idea after not eating all day. She didn't move and closed her eyes again, turning her head away and slowly rolling so her back was to him. She didn't care what Spence thought or wanted. She was staying right here.

His hand, with its smooth—but not girlie—palm, rested against her forehead as she tried to move farther away.

"No fever," he grunted.

"You woke me out of a sound sleep."

"I wouldn't have woken you if you'd been in the bed."

"I was comfortable here."

"I'll help you to bed."

"You will not. I'm staying here."

"Olympia, I'm not letting you sleep here. Come on." She turned enough to see him towering over the couch, his arms crossed over his chest—his broad chest, where she'd laid her cheek after they'd made love.

"Go away." She squinched her eyes closed against him and the memories of that night. Dear Lord, the night she'd gotten pregnant. Her stomach heaved, and she fought her way out of her nest of pillows.

When she finally came out of the bathroom, she didn't fight Spence as he helped her to the bed. Exhausted, she just wanted to lie down and have her head stop spinning. Spence held up the covers for her, and she carefully slid in. She lay there in the middle of the huge empty bed, listening to him in the bathroom, brushing his teeth and doing all those domestic things that she'd imagined in her silly girlhood would mean that she finally belonged somewhere and to someone. Now here she was, married to a man she didn't like most hours of the day, pregnant—there, she'd thought it without hyperventilating—and alone on her wedding night.

Tears tracked down her cheeks. She wiped at them and buried her face farther into the pillow. She hated crying but couldn't stop the sob that bubbled up and out. She tightened her jaw to keep the next one in. Her chest hurt from holding back her gasping breaths. Her eyes burned from the tears, then the sob parted her lips and she couldn't stop. What the hell was she crying about? The bed dipped. She popped up, wrestling with the blankets and sheets.

"Everything's okay," Spence whispered, brushing

her hair behind her ear. "Lie down." He pulled her toward him, bringing her cheek to rest on that solid chest, where she could hear the thud of his heart. His hand rubbed her back. She wanted to tell him to get away from her. Instead, she lay there, clutching his shirt and blubbering. Damn it. She wasn't the kind of woman who cried. She'd always prided herself on that.

Hours passed. It had to be hours. Her tears left tight, salty trails on her cheeks. Her eyelids rasped across her eyes. She tried to push herself away from Spence, but he just tightened his hold.

"Relax. Go to sleep. Morning will be here before we know it."

Even those inane words made her feel better as she drifted into sleep, thinking that this would be something to tell their children. She jerked awake. She wasn't keeping the baby, and she wasn't keeping Spence. None of that was in the life she had planned. James women made horrible wives and even worse mothers.

THE COMBINATION OF a vibrating pocket and deliciously round female butt against his crotch brought Spence slowly and pleasantly from sleep as an imaginary Olympia asked him, "Is that your phone? Or are you just happy to feel me?"

The vibration paused for five breaths as he gathered himself to figure out where he was and why his mouth tasted as if he'd eaten dead coyote for dinner. He rolled slowly away from Olympia. His wife. Had he really married her? Had they really gotten pregnant? Was that the sun coming in through the curtains?

He sat up slowly, making sure he didn't jar his head. He knew that once he really woke up, the hangover he deserved would pierce his brain. "Hello," he whispered hoarsely into the phone.

"Daddy," Calvin said. "You forgot to call."

Spence stood quickly and hustled from the bed to the window. Crap. The sun was bright and way up in the sky. Then the spike-through-the-head hangover hit. Why had he sucked down four whiskeys? Whiskey always gave him a bad hangover. "Calvin…" Spence started, then cleared his throat. "I'm sorry, buddy. I got busy."

"You're always busy. When are you going to come and get me? I don't want to live here anymore."

Spence choked on his response. Calvin actually sounded cranky, like a normal little boy. Not the quiet and older-than-his-years boy who'd learned tough lessons from his years of illness. His son's idea of defiance was not putting his LEGOs away. "We've got to talk to the judge—"

"He's a poopy head."

Spence stifled a laugh to stop the tears. He wanted Calvin with him now. Not months from now when the legal system figured out that Spence was the boy's father and the person who had the "greatest concern for his physical and emotional well-being." He dug deep for his calm, firm dad voice. "That's not nice. He's the judge, and we've got to listen to what he says. It won't be long."

"Uh-oh." Calvin's voice dropped to a whisper. "Grandma…Mimi is in the hall. Bye, Daddy."

Spence's knuckles turned white as he fought the urge to hurl the phone across the room. Just the sound of Calvin's grandma in the hall was enough to send the boy running. He didn't know how Calvin had found a phone to use, but his son clearly needed to talk with him. When he calmed down, he'd call and ask to speak with the little boy. Hopefully, Eugenia and Stuart Smythe-Ferris—the pretentious last name Missy was back to using—would be open to a brief conversation, despite being sticklers for following every comma of the custody agreement.

He glanced over at Olympia, who'd scooted into the divot made by his body. She didn't look close to waking up. Wasn't she a cowgirl? Weren't they up at the crack of dawn? The only other cowgirl he knew was his sister-in-law, Jessie, and she was out in the barn before the sun rose most days.

He moved to the in-room coffeepot to brew something to combat the headache. They needed to get on the road because he had to be at the office by noon. He'd given some crap-ass excuse to get the time off. No one at the office knew about his marriage, except HR.

"Olympia," he said more sharply than he'd meant to. She jerked.

"Wha—?" she mumbled, her head coming up, then falling back down with a thump.

"It's nearly checkout time, and I've got to get to the office."

Olympia squeezed her eyes shut and moaned.

Crap. She was going to be sick. Sympathy jabbed at his conscience. After all, it was his baby making her so ill. He said calmly, "There's soda there for your stomach."

She climbed out of the bed and slammed into the bathroom. He heard retching. He refocused on the coffeepot, watching with extreme concentration the drip of the magical brew. His head pounded, but the first slug of coffee would help.

"Olympia," he called through the closed door. "Are you okay? I need to use the bathroom, and we've got to get going."

"I'm not going anywhere. I'm going to die." She groaned.

"Try the soda." He cared about how she felt, really he did, but work was waiting and so was convincing his ex in-laws that he had to talk with Calvin today. The anxious tone of his son's voice played again in his mind.

"Maybe ginger ale?"

"I'm going downstairs to get one."

How had his simple plan spiraled so out of control? he asked himself as he searched through the overpriced convenience store in the lobby for ginger ale. He could feel the time ticking away. Finally, he paid the three dollars for a bottle and made his way back upstairs in the world's slowest elevator.

"Got the ginger ale," he said as he opened the door. The room was quiet. He walked through and saw the bathroom door was open. "Olympia?"

She was back in bed, with the covers over her head.

"Olympia, we've got to go. You can sleep in the truck." She shook her head like a toddler. He didn't have time for this. He yanked all the covers off. "Let's go."

"If I get in your truck, I'll be sick."

"Drink this," he said, holding out the soda. She cracked open one eye, then held out her hand for the bottle. She sat up slowly. He wanted to tell her to hurry, but he also didn't want her back in the bathroom. "While you drink that, I'll get ready. Five minutes."

She was sitting propped against the pillows when

he came out of the bathroom, about half the soda gone. Her just-below-the-chin, deep brunette hair was messy, and dark circles still ringed her eyes, but she no longer looked whiter than the sheets.

"Good. You're ready."

He refilled his coffee and shoved their stuff into the duffel. They had to get going now.

"Just leave me here."

"Can't afford the room for another night." He opened the dresser drawers, looking for any stray items.

"I'll be sick again."

"You have the ginger ale, and I'll stop at a drive-thru for breakfast. You need food."

"I'll get a taxi and meet you at the ranch."

"No taxi will take you that far out of town."

Olympia curled into a ball. "No."

He'd had less trouble with Calvin when he was little. "Olympia, I will carry you downstairs if I have to. We're going."

She sighed dramatically and slowly sat up. "If I get sick, it's your fault."

"I'm willing to take the risk."

Olympia walked over to him, pushing at her hair. "Okay. I'm ready."

"You're going in that?"

"What does it matter? We're just headed home."

"Don't you, um, want to…well, maybe…a bra?"

She glanced down. "What? Nothing's showing, is it?"

Was she making a joke? He could see her nipples and the generous curve of her breasts! He could imagine them filling his hands, soft but firm. He dug in the duffel and pushed her bra at her. His face had to be red.

The last time he'd blushed about a girl's bra had been in the eighth grade.

"I need to wash my face, too." She strolled to the bathroom with her bra hooked on her finger. Was she putting an extra swing in her walk?

Spence adjusted his stance, wishing that his hangover was worse, bad enough that all he could think about was the pounding pain in his head. Instead, he remembered holding on to those hips as… He refocused his inner dialogue, telling himself to check the room for more of their stuff. Think about Calvin. Recite legal code. Remember what it felt like when he turned eighteen and his parents, who were on a cruise, didn't even call to wish him a happy birthday. That did it. Calvin would never know that kind of disappointment and hurt.

Chapter Four

Olympia's touchy stomach growled when she got a deep whiff of the smell of cumin, chili and sizzling meat that hung over the restaurant. Good thing because if she'd run to the bathroom, Spence's very smart doctor brother would figure out everything. Her stomach did a tiny flip as she thought about the pages that Spence had proposed adding to their prenup to "address the ongoing custody and care of any issue of said marriage" after they'd discovered she was pregnant last week.

"So how're things going? That rescue horse working out?" her new brother-in-law asked. "Jessie wanted me to find out." Payson was as tall as Spence but a little thinner and much darker. She wondered how two brothers from the same parents could look so different.

"He's doing fine. I'm getting him sorted out. Why couldn't Jessie come with you?" She hoped she didn't sound desperate. Being surrounded by MacCormack men made her nervous.

"She has a new crop of therapists to introduce today. But I'm supposed to warn you that we'll be down to see you before I fly back to Philadelphia."

"I thought you were done with the East Coast?" Olympia swallowed hard and told her brain to calm down. Getting him to talk about his program at Children's Hospital would stop him from focusing on her. Could he see the pregnancy glow or something?

"Not yet," Payson said. "My contract with Children's runs through the end of next year. Even with a lawyer in the family, I couldn't get out of it. Jessie and I keep reminding ourselves that it'll be over soon. Plus, she's so busy, she doesn't notice whether I'm there or not." Payson's smile moved only the very corners of his mouth.

"That's not true and you know it," Spence said. "Plus, how are you two supposed to give Calvin a little cousin if you aren't even in the same state?"

Olympia wanted to kick Spence. How dare he talk about pregnancy and babies? He'd promised her that he wouldn't say a word tonight about the baby, but had added that they couldn't keep the pregnancy secret forever.

"I don't need a birds-and-bees talk from my little brother," Payson said with a slight edge as his smile disappeared.

Olympia felt Spence stiffen beside her. She dug her hand into his thigh as the increased tension went right to her now-unsettled stomach. How could she endure months of sickness?

Spence relaxed just a fraction and answered in his cowboy drawl, "Well, there, pardner, just wanted to make sure y'all know how it's done."

She scrambled to say something that would get the two of them off this path. "I heard Molly is getting her own YouTube channel? *Pony Diva?* Or is it *Pony Princess*?" Payson finally relaxed and actually smiled.

"That pony already had a swelled head. The video of her at our wedding got ten thousand hits." He shook his head. "The kids bring their phones and tablets, take videos of her, upload them and then show them to her. I swear she watches."

"If she needs an agent, tell Jessie to give me a call," Spence said just as the waitress came to the table with their order.

Olympia surveyed her meal. Soup and salad. Nothing spicy. Nothing with any flavor. She still wasn't sure if she could eat it and keep it down. Her soda had stayed put, so she lifted a spoonful of the broth. At the same time, Spence raised an overflowing burrito to his mouth. She caught a whiff of chili and beef. Nausea rose, then his arm brushed the side of her breast, causing her nipple to tighten. Her body didn't know whether to be sick or get ready to do the nasty. She jerked away and spilled a little soup.

Payson's gaze zeroed in on her.

She put her head down. She had to stay calm in order to keep from racing to the bathroom. She wasn't ready—and might never be ready—for Payson and Jessie to know about the baby. Which was totally stupid because unless she went somewhere far away, everyone would know she was pregnant eventually. She pushed her meal away. Spence gave her the stink eye, but she didn't care.

"Something wrong with the food?" Payson asked, a forkful of tamales on the way to his mouth, dripping with guacamole and salsa verde. She averted her eyes from the green goo.

"I had a big lunch."

He ate his bite and gave her another long stare. "So you're boarding horses and rescues at the ranch…where my brother is currently living?"

"Ha-ha," Spence said. "I know you and Jessie think it's hilarious that I'm living on a ranch, but if it gets me Calvin, I'd even clean the stalls."

"You think this'll work?"

Spence nodded and talked about the custody. All she could think was, *My baby will have a big brother*. Olympia gulped down nausea. Spence turned to her, his hand going—without her permission—to her abdomen. Her head swiveled sharply. She caught Payson looking at them with speculation. Damn it. Now was not the time for this.

"I've got animals to take care of. We almost ready?" She knew how rude she sounded. She didn't care. When she was outside, the hot dry air settled her down by short-circuiting the rush of fear that hit her when she imagined Payson asking what she and Spence were hiding. What would they tell him? Jessie? They knew the marriage was a sham.

TWO DAYS AFTER the near disaster of a dinner, Olympia visited Muffin, the rescue that Jessie had recently asked her to take on. The horse, true to form, backed away from her, teeth bared. The paint gelding had bad habits and a quick temper—probably abused in his past. He was wary of humans, and the feeling was mutual. He'd bitten Olympia three times and stomped her foot. Her ranch was home to him and three other horses, not enough to cover the bills since only two were paying customers.

"Seven months, Muffin. I can do this for seven months. Otherwise no feed for you." In a little over half a year, she'd have the baby, and…she'd be free of Spence and ready to hit the rodeo circuit. No way would she feel sad about leaving her fake cowboy. Plus, Rickie would have the cash she needed for school. She smiled thinking about her sister, with her red hair and long legs—nothing like Olympia. Made sense for her and Rickie, since they only shared James DNA. Olympia vaguely remembered Rickie's slow-talking dad, an Oklahoma cowboy who hadn't stuck around for his daughter's birth.

While she and Spence lived together, money should be a little less tight. Olympia might be able to figure out a way to trade for or get the funds to buy a barrel racer. Then she'd be ready to hit the circuit running—so to speak. *Right, cowgirl, and exactly how are you going to practice with a big old belly?*

Muffin shook his head, his mane going in six directions. Olympia smiled at the gelding's goofiness and not just the fact that the less-than-pleasant animal had been given such a girlie handle. Jessie said that he'd been named for his unnatural love of muffins—butter-rum ones, in particular. She wasn't ready to break down and bribe him with those treats…yet. She reached over the stall to put the bucket of feed in place. Muffin showed his teeth. "Silly horse," Olympia said. "Biting the hand that feeds you is a bad idea." She checked his water, then moved on to the boarders.

Now what? All the chores were done, and she might actually be hungry. She'd have to face the house sometime.

"Dinner, Olympia," Spence said from the barn door.

She whipped around but could see only his silhouette against the setting sun, his hat cocked at an angle that gave her a shiver of recognition. He looked just like a cowboy who'd be the sort of stand-up guy she could rely on and fall in love with. But that had been the dream of a teenager. She didn't want to feel that for Spence or the instant flash of heat. So she'd lie and tell him she wasn't hungry. Then what? She couldn't sleep in the barn. She'd agreed to marry him and live with him. Time to act like a civilized human being. "What are we having?"

"Chicken fingers and fries."

She stared at him, trying to decide if he was making a joke.

He stared back. "It's Calvin's favorite. I'm missing him."

She waited for him to say more, but when he didn't, she replied, "As long as I don't have to cook it, I'm good."

"My cooking skills are limited, but I can make a meal. Are you ready?"

"I'm done, and I might even be hungry."

"Are these your horses for racing?"

"No. I'm boarding those two." She waved to the closest animals. "Pasquale there is a rescue that…well, he just never left. The one at the far end is another rescue Jessie talked me into taking. If I was a little more centrally located, it'd be simpler to board more animals. It's just too far for most people."

"It is way out. Family ranch?"

"You could say that." She didn't want to talk about the father who'd given her the property in apology for a lifetime of neglect.

"So your family is from Arizona?"

He was making polite conversation. She could return the favor. She might have grown up like trailer trash, but she'd learned a lot since then. "My sisters and I grew up over near Bisbee."

"Sisters. You have more than Rickie, right?"

"Two others. They're between me and Rickie."

"What'd you tell them about the wedding?"

"Nothing. They'll just assume I hitched my wagon to yours for the cash. That's what we James women do. Find a sugar daddy." Olympia tried to smile and make a joke of it. That wasn't easy since her entire life she'd been telling herself that she'd never get stuck pregnant and relying on a man like her mama and grammy. She and Spence stood in the doorway, and even over the horses and hay, she could smell him—which would have been fine, except it made her warm and gooey inside. "I'm hungry," she said, hoping that would encourage him to move on.

"That's good. If you can't keep down food, there could be trouble for the baby."

"Thought your brother was the doctor?" She followed Spence to the house, taking sneak peeks at the way his jeans followed the curve of his rear. They wouldn't be sleeping together again—because that would just be a bad idea, right?—but she could still admire the view. She'd had that strong, round butt in her hands when Spence had… When they'd made the baby that… Damn. The nausea roiled up from her middle. "I'm going to skip dinner," she said, rushing by him and into her room.

She sat on her bed, closing her eyes and willing away the ball of sickness. Could she break the contract? Hide out somewhere until she had the baby and handed it over to a nice couple? If she'd had a normal family, she would've been on the phone to her mama for advice and support. She'd never had the time to make close friends, either, because she'd been taking care of her siblings. Who had time for going to dances or sleepovers when her sisters were at home sick with the flu? She'd barely squeaked through high school. For a second, she thought about calling Jessie, but her one friend was also Spence's sister-in-law—hers, too, she guessed. That meant Olympia couldn't confide in her, could she? No. That would put Jessie in a bad place.

"YOU'VE GOT TO EAT," Spence said through the door, hoping his voice sounded less annoyed than he felt.

"Not now."

"Come on. What can I make you? Toast?"

The door swung open, and he stepped back from Olympia's white and angry face. "I'm not hungry. If I eat anything, I'll throw up. I do not like throwing up, so I'm not eating. I might not be a smart attorney, but I can figure that out on my own."

"You might be nauseated because you haven't eaten. Everything I've read indicates that having frequent small amounts of food will stop the queasy feeling." She clenched her fists, and his internal voice said, *You had to prove that you're smarter, didn't you?*

"Do you want me to kill you?"

He backed away. "If you don't want supper, we still need to talk." She didn't move. "Um, I've addressed your concerns with the…" He motioned to her midsection.

"Adoption, like I asked?"

"How many times do I have to tell you? I don't walk away from my children." She glared at him as color flooded her unnaturally pale cheeks. He went on, "The document makes it clear that you won't be responsible for the child."

"Fine. But I don't want a bunch of legalese crap. I don't have the money for a lawyer to check on you." She gulped in a breath.

"Are you going to be sick?"

"Probably." She closed her eyes, and any color she'd gained disappeared.

He reached out to touch her but let his hand hover. They didn't have that kind of relationship. He really didn't have the right to comfort her. But he couldn't stop feeling that he should hold her until she felt like her usual sassy, drive-him-to-drink self. "We can do this later if you need to lie down." His fingers landed lightly on her forearm. He could feel the warmth of her skin under his fingertips and the slight tremor. He aimed her toward the twin bed shoved against the wall. What the hell? She hadn't let him into the spare room she'd taken when he moved in. It was so tiny. Why had she insisted he take the master bedroom and its big bed? "Come on. Get in. I'll finish the draft and leave it for you to read on your own. It's about protecting you, too." He worried when she dropped onto the bed, letting her head hang forward.

"If you say so," she whispered.

"I say so." He knelt in front of her and pulled off her sneakers. He liked the boots better. He'd like to see her in nothing but those boots. *Whoa.* That was not what he wanted and definitely not what they needed. What was wrong with him? She was sick. She wasn't really his wife. More important, she didn't even like him.

When her shoes were off, she curled into a ball on the bed. "Go away. I want to die on my own."

"You won't die," he said softly. "It's morning sickness. It'll go away."

"Is it morning?"

"Just a turn of phrase. The nausea can happen at any time of day. Researchers believe that it's a warning system. That usually the illness is triggered by foods that could cause the baby harm."

"Toast? Toast is harmful?"

"It's not a perfect system." He smiled at her tousled hair. He wanted to smooth the strands to comfort her, except the other feelings that had him shifting on his feet had nothing to do with tenderness. *Stop it, you perv.* "It'll get better. It always does."

"I'm holding you to that."

He stood for another moment, imagining their baby…his baby. Good Lord, he was going to be a father again. He hurried out of the room, so he didn't do something stupid like cry or give her a hug.

THE SOUND OF Olympia being sick on the other side of the door ratcheted up Spence's worry. They'd been at the ranch for three weeks, and Olympia had been sick nearly 24/7…although that hadn't stopped her from going out to the barn or looking for more horses to board and train.

Fear sweat gathered in his armpits. Could a woman die from morning sickness? He'd looked it up on Google. He pulled out his phone. Hey, he had a doctor in the family. He dialed Payson. Where was his brother, Arizona or Philadelphia?

"What?" Payson asked, sounding harried and annoyed.

"Olympia is pregnant and has been throwing up constantly," Spence spewed out, the fear choking his voice a little as Olympia moaned in distress. "Do I need to take her to the emergency room?"

"Excuse me?"

"Do I need to take Olympia to the ER?"

"I can't get past *pregnant*. Your phony wife is pregnant?"

"Yes," Spence said, realizing this had been a huge mistake. He'd called on instinct, not with the thinking part of his brain. "I'll just take her to one of those clinics. Never mind."

"Don't hang up," Payson said. "Olympia is having a baby. I thought you said this wasn't a real marriage?"

"Pregnancy and marriage are not correlated."

"I know that, but—"

"It's your fault. Well, yours and Jessie's."

"I don't see how. You might be a lawyer, but even you've got to understand basic anatomy—"

"Ha-ha. Very funny. She's sick constantly. I swear she's lost twenty pounds."

"I doubt she's lost that much weight. I want to understand how she got pregnant when you've been married for less than a month."

"We met at your wedding."

"You hooked up at our wedding? Were you so drunk that you didn't—"

"The condom broke."

"You're sure it's your baby? It seems awfully convenient that you offer her a marriage proposal with money… I assume you offered her money, since you told me you might have to sell that damned truck, which you love better than any man should."

"The baby is mine." Spence made himself loosen his

grip on the phone. Olympia wasn't that kind of woman, which he'd known even before she'd punched him. She lived by a cowgirl code like his sister-in-law's. No matter what she might say about walking away from the baby and her family, she was the one who'd stepped in when her youngest sister lost her scholarship. "I didn't call you for a lecture. I called you for medical advice. Second, Olympia didn't know she was pregnant when Elvis married us."

"Really? An adult woman didn't put together that she'd had sex, then didn't have her period? Pregnancy never came to mind?"

"Do I need to take her somewhere?" Spence asked, listening intently at the bathroom door. Silence. Had she passed out?

"If you think she's dehydrated, yes. Otherwise, make an appointment as soon as possible." Payson's voice was coldly clinical. "You know it's not your job to save her, right?"

"That's your thing, Payson. I have a prenup contract with her, and it's all about keeping Calvin safe. I'll do whatever it takes. Right now, I'm married, and my wife is pregnant."

"Not your wife, the woman who you talked into acting as your wife. Remember that."

Spence hung up and stared at the closed door. He raised his hand, letting it hover there for a moment before tapping lightly. "Olympia, you okay?"

A choked "Fine" came through the closed door.

"Open up, so I know for sure."

"No," Olympia said, her voice stronger. Water ran in the sink, making the old-as-dirt pipes clatter. The house had been built by someone with enthusiasm but a definite lack of skill. Nothing worked well, and everything needed to be updated, including the bathroom.

"Let me get you some—"

The door opened, and Olympia stood there, swaying just a little, dark circles under her eyes, her lips bloodless. "I'm fine."

"If by *fine*, you mean that you could audition to be one of the walking dead…" His heart beat hard in his chest. "We're going to the ER."

"Absolutely not," she said, her knuckles white as her hand gripped the jamb, her jaw thrust forward. They'd been living together long enough for him to know what that meant. A boulder would be easier to move. A stupid part of him admired her grit. "You're going to the doctor tomorrow."

"I have an appointment."

"For next week. That's too far away. I'll call from the office, and if that doesn't work, then I'll get Payson to call them."

Olympia had just opened her mouth when crickets sounded from her pocket. She pulled out the phone and narrowed her tabby-cat eyes at him in an obvious this-conversation-is-not-done look. "Hey, Jessie, what's up?" She took a small step from the door. He didn't walk away. Her paleness worried him. He didn't want to leave her alone until she was in bed or sitting on the couch. "Payson told you what?"

Apparently, doctor-patient privacy didn't count when it was your brother.

"Yeah. That night. I can't talk about it now. I've got to go." Olympia shoved the phone into her jeans' pocket and turned slowly to him. "You told your brother? We decided to keep it quiet until we worked everything out."

"I called him for medical advice. I wanted to know about morning sickness."

"Get that damned agreement out now because we're going to hammer this out. I don't want any more surprises."

"You do know that eventually everyone will know you're pregnant."

"We'd better be divorced before then."

He opened his mouth to tell her that if anyone really looked at her now, they'd know. He glanced down where her shirt stretched across her breasts. The generous curves had swelled to… She crossed her arms over her chest and glared at him. He said hastily, "I'll get you toast and soda, then we'll talk about the prenup."

"I'll meet you in the kitchen."

Chapter Five

Pausing their discussion and moving to the kitchen had gotten rid of any sense of emotional connection, Olympia decided. She sat on the mismatched chair at the table she'd salvaged from a pile of trash left on the side of the road. She'd slapped a heavy coat of sunny-yellow paint on it, which had turned it into a blinding rectangle rather than a "sunny accent." Maybe she should start buying women's magazines rather than *Barrel Racer News* and *Ranchers Monthly*. The place still needed those homey touches that seemed beyond her. On the other hand, she had zero dollars to make it any better. On the third hand, she'd always lived with zero dollars. Would that ever change? She swallowed hard, heartburn adding to her misery. How could she even have heartburn when she'd eaten nothing?

"What?" Spence asked staring at her hard from where he stood at the cupboard.

"TUMS. I need TUMS."

"Stay there. I'll get them."

Olympia fought to keep her head up so she wouldn't knock it against the table, weeping. Because she felt like crap…all the damn—darn—time…and because her rodeo dreams and freedom from her never-ending, crushing responsibilities felt further and further away. Worse, she'd gotten harnessed to a man who would leave as soon as he got his son, no matter what he said about family. She knew how this story would end, with her holding a baby and watching him walk away—like every other man in her life.

He stood above her holding out the plastic container of TUMS. His dusty-blue eyes were marred by a shadow of worry and something she couldn't quite name. She took the bottle, careful to not touch him. She'd learned in their weeks together that even brushing up against him made her shivery and hot. It had to be the pregnancy that had turned her into a heap of exposed nerve endings.

He produced a yellow legal pad from somewhere. She never imagined that lawyers actually used them.

"The current agreement is clear about how we'll dissolve the marriage, but it didn't take into account—" he hesitated "—a pregnancy, as you know."

"I didn't imagine being pregnant."

"I know. That's what we're trying to address."

She nodded and stopped as her head swam. Women actually wanted to get pregnant? Her mama had done this four times! If she'd had a different relationship—really, any relationship—with her mother, she'd call and ask when the sickness went away. Jessie had been pregnant once and was trying again, but because she'd lost the first baby, the subject was too sensitive to ask her for advice or even sympathy. "What did you say?"

"I said I want you to sign over full custody of the baby to me in utero."

"Excuse me?"

"I want it to be clear that the baby is mine since its conception."

"There you go again, getting all puffed up about your damned…darned swimmers."

"No," he said, his eyes glued on the notepad. "I just want to make sure that no matter what happens over the next few months, my interests in the baby are clear."

"You know that the baby is a human being, not a truck?"

"I know better than you what it means to have a baby."

"Because you got some other woman pregnant? She's trying to keep you from that kid. Doesn't seem as if you know much." She didn't even know what words were coming out of her mouth. Was she trying to wound him? She looked across the crappy table at her attorney "husband" with his cowboy pearl-snap shirt and Piaget watch. She flushed with annoyance at his cowboy fakery and the whole danged situation.

"You've said you don't want the baby. I'm ensuring that it is clear that custody has been transferred to me. What do you care, as long as you're not responsible, darlin'?" His mouth held no hint of a good-time-cowboy smile, and his eyes—definitely sharky now—were flat and opaque.

His attitude and tone elevated her heartburn from two-alarm to five. She dug another TUMS out of the bottle. "I want to give the baby up for adoption, to a family that will…well… She doesn't want me as a mother anyway, and how exactly are you going to keep her from knowing who I am when—"

"If that's all you're worried about, I can write into the agreement that your name will be expunged from all the records. There'll be no mention of the child in the divorce. We'll do it in a separate closed agreement."

Olympia nodded. Suddenly, the idea of her baby never knowing her made her heart hurt. That had to be just the hormones. Olympia knew her future; it wasn't here with Spence and kids. The rodeo. Barrel racing. Seeing the world. Yep. That was where she was headed. Her hand crept to her belly, but she pulled it away. She knew where a baby led—directly to a broken-down trailer and handouts. Before she could change her mind, she said, "Write that in there, that you'll never reveal the mother's name. Never."

"If that's what you want." He looked at her strangely but made notes on his pad. "Even if I get custody of Calvin before the baby is born, I will expect us to remain together."

"Absolutely not. I won't be here with your son."

"It's not the best situation because I certainly don't want him to get the idea that he's got a new mother. But I need to be there for the baby." He nodded toward her belly.

"How did this get so complicated?"

"Darlin', it got complicated the minute I took you out onto the dance floor."

Olympia's heart thudded a little harder, remembering their slow dance. Their hips brushing against each other, her snuggling into his shoulder and then his hands roaming over her body. From that one dance, they'd quickly ended up in her room and then… Well, it had been… Nope. She wasn't going to think about that night because it was the whole reason for the complication right now. "That's not happening again. We have a business arrangement."

"As you pointed out, we're talking about a baby, not a truck."

"Not yet. This is just a…peanut." She pointed at her stomach. The situation still didn't feel totally real— even with the morning sickness and the overflowing cups on her bra.

"You look as though you've got more than a peanut going on," Spence said, staring where her T-shirt strained to cover her chest.

Sharp heat filled her breasts, making her nipples harden and the space between her thighs soften. "I…" The heat moved to her face. She didn't know whether to be turned on, embarrassed or pissed off. She opened her mouth again to say…what? She had no idea.

His hand moved to grasp hers as he half stood and leaned forward. She had plenty of time to pull back. Instead, she acted like a little mouse mesmerized by a snake. She sat while his softly curved lips came closer and closer. They touched hers, moved over them, nibbling until she opened her mouth on a gasp as warmth tingled from her lips throughout her body. She wanted to taste the licorice and excitement of him. She wanted to feel again that sexy connection they'd shared months ago. The one she still felt when he looked at her or brushed past her. He pulled her to her feet and against him. She didn't even know how it had happened. She reveled in the sexiness of the kiss, the gut-level primitive need she had for him.

Spence cradled her head. He wanted to taste every nuance of her lovely mouth. The one that made him hot and angry at the same time. Hot when he noticed the soft curve of her lip. Angry when she spewed…who the hell cared what. His free hand moved to her breast, gently cupping the heavier, new weight of it. That wasn't enough. He heard her whimper and knew that sound. She'd made a similar demand when she'd urged him to take her in that motel room. His hand clawed at the edge of her T-shirt, pulling it up so his hand could be flesh to flesh with her breast. "Oh, dear Lord," he gasped against her mouth. The contact aroused him. He moved his hips against her, torturing himself with the warm curves of her hips.

"Spence…what…are we doing?" Olympia half moaned, her hands both pulling and pushing at him. She didn't know what she wanted. Her body wanted him right here on the kitchen table. A moan started from deep inside as his hand—when did he get so many of them?—snaked into the unbuttoned top of her jeans, pushing open her zipper so his fingers could tease her. "Jeez…what are you—?"

"I'm givin' my cowgirl the ride of her life," Spence said, his breath warming her ear as his fingers explored her.

"Stop talking. I don't—"

His mouth covered hers as he touched her. Her hands fumbled for the snap on his pants, opening it so she could reach down to cup his muscled, taut butt. She pulled him tight against her, trapping his hand and rocking. His fingers moved a fraction of an inch, and she flew apart. She slumped against him, and Spence whispered, "I've got you, cowgirl. I'll always have you."

His words startled her, and she pulled away. The rush of cool air brought her back to her senses. Oh, my God. What had she just done? In her kitchen. She stepped back, noticing now that her pants were around her thighs. Spence's were open and she could see the bulge in his tighty whities. Dear Lord. She needed to get out of here. After racing to the bathroom as she pulled up her jeans, she sat down on the floor and leaned against the small tub, its cool porcelain soothing her hot skin. She'd just used Spence like a sex toy. Where was that in their agreement?

SPENCE DREW IN deep breaths as he leaned on the table, willing his pulse to stop racing. What had they just done? What they probably shouldn't have. He sucked in a final deep breath, stood fully and finally noticed his pants were undone. He gingerly zipped up the jeans, telling himself that no man had died from a raging hard-on. The yellow legal pad sat on the table. That was what he should be concentrating on, instead of Olympia's uninhibited response. He shifted as he was rubbed uncomfortably by his confining Ariats

He went to the refrigerator for a beer and heard Olympia's bedroom door close. Good. This would give him a chance to cool down and figure out what would happen next. He gulped at the beer. By the time half the bottle was gone, he had himself under control. He got his laptop so he could answer emails and work on the Texas case he'd been assigned.

But he couldn't concentrate. Was that a noise from Olympia's bedroom? Had she gotten worse? He hesitated for a moment, talking himself into believing the sounds had been a figment of his imagination, fueled by the unfinished business in the kitchen. This time he was sure he heard a noise. He hurried down the short, dark hall, stood for two seconds outside her closed door, then knocked and opened it in the same motion.

"What?" Olympia asked as she grasped at a T-shirt

to cover herself, which hadn't stopped him from catching a glimpse of the glowing whiteness of her breasts or the deep, darkness of her nipples. He didn't stop his forward momentum.

"I heard you."

"I was… I couldn't find a shirt that fit right." Dusky rose stained the lightly tanned skin of her cheeks.

"Oh," he said lamely. He reached out his hand. He had to feel again the soft weight, the taut response of the nipple, hear the moan as he rubbed—

"Stop—" Olympia choked out. He didn't stop pushing aside the shirt.

He looked at her face, amazed that his hand had followed his imagination without direction from his brain. "I can't. I've just got to… There." His hand settled against her breast, the heat of her warming his palm. Olympia took a hesitant step forward.

"Harder," she whispered leaning into him. "I need… Touch me…harder."

He pulled her to him, his hands firmly taking her breast and her butt so that she stretched against him in a tight line.

"Kiss me," Olympia heard herself say in a husky voice that wasn't hers. She should be embarrassed, but she wanted the sizzling link they'd shared on the table. She wanted all of him this time. His breathing went ragged as she pushed his jeans and underwear down. He stepped out of them and settled himself between her thighs. "I get to have a little fun first." Holding his weight on his arms, he brushed his lips against hers, enjoying their sweetness as she tried to deepen the kiss. "Not yet. I want to savor this."

"Hell no," Olympia said, wrapping her arms around him, yanking him down onto her.

"I'll squash you."

"Is that what you call it now?" she laughed, husky and sexy.

Before her laugh finished, he'd reversed their positions and now she lay stretched out over him. "You're a cowgirl, right? Prove it. Ride a cowboy. Save a horse."

"You got that right, cowboy." Olympia rocked her hips forward as he entered her. Quickly, she found a rhythm, reveling in her body's power. She barely heard Spence urging her on as her climax broke over her once again, and his hips lifted off the bed in a squeal of springs.

"That's how we break in cowboys around here," she whispered against his sweaty neck, savoring the closeness of him, the safety his very presence gave her, allowing her to fall asleep in one swift blink.

Chapter Six

Light seeped through the partially open curtains. A lot of light. Olympia burst from the sheets and immediately flopped back onto the bed as sickness crept up the back of her throat. What time was it? She reached out for the phone on her nightstand—9:00 a.m. Spence had left hours ago for work. She had to get up now and take care of the animals. Muffin would be knocking down his stall for his morning feed. There were the others to take care of, plus she had a potential client coming to check out the barn for her animal.

She stared at the ceiling as she considered what had happened last night. She could blame the constant sickness, saying it'd eaten away at the thinking part of her brain, but she wasn't a liar. She'd wanted him last night. This morning? Pretty much the same, except the nausea was back. Maybe sex was what she needed to combat the sickness?

She slid out of bed, standing carefully and not moving until she felt settled. Her room looked fine, but the faint scent of licorice and sex made her thighs tighten in remembered pleasure. She refused to be disappointed that Spence hadn't woken her like Sleeping Beauty this morning. Of course, saying she was Sleeping Beauty might be a stretch. *Get into the shower*, she told herself firmly. *Wash off his scent and cowgirl up.* Whether they should or shouldn't do a repeat of last night—she certainly hoped they would for the sake of her morning sickness—right now, she had chores to do.

Moving in slow motion, Olympia got through her barn work and dragged herself back to the house. She slid open the back door, which led directly into the kitchen, and screamed.

Another feminine screech filled the room. "You scared the crap out of me," accused her youngest sister.

"Rickie! What are you doing here? Aren't you supposed to be in school?"

"Nah. Classes don't start for weeks. Mama is being a pain, and Grammy moved back in after her latest boyfriend dumped her. I had to get out of there. Can I stay here?"

Olympia's stomach, which *had* settled nicely, went into a churning wave of sickness. "No," she gasped and hurried to the bathroom where she threw up the juice and Gatorade she'd sipped in the barn. The pounding on the bathroom door finally registered on her sluggish brain. She had to get herself together before she faced her sister. She rinsed her mouth, looked at herself in the mirror and considered makeup to hide how rough she looked. No. Then Rickie would know something was wrong. "What?" Olympia asked belligerently as she yanked open the door. A good offense was being offensive, she'd learned in a house full of females.

"What do you mean *what*? You're sick. Do you have the flu? Or is it—?"

"Flu. You'd better stay away. Maybe you shouldn't crash here."

Rickie shook her head, her jaw thrusting out just like Olympia knew her own did. "I can't leave you here by yourself."

Olympia didn't resist when Rickie led her down the hall. "The other bedroom," she told her sister, directing her away from the master bedroom—the one that had been Olympia's before Spence had moved in. Since she hadn't told her sister or anyone else in her family about the marriage or about Spence, how could she explain his presence there or in other places in the house, where he'd made himself at home for nearly a month? Her head swam a little, making it hard to concentrate. Did her room still smell like him and sex? Why hadn't they gone to his room with its big bed?

Rickie topped Olympia by a good four or five inches and liked to loom over her, like a bosomy sequoia. "What was wrong with your old bedroom?" Rickie didn't move, and Olympia kept her mouth closed. "I'll bring you cinnamon toast and chocolate milk."

Tears stung Olympia's eyelids. That was what she'd always brought the girls when they didn't feel good. She nodded and watched Rickie amble out of the room. Her sister never hurried. Her father had been a true cowboy from Oklahoma who'd passed through their lives like a slow summer breeze. Olympia had liked him, but Papa Don had left like all the other men. He sent birthday cards…some years.

No rehashing the past. She had to focus on the here and now. What would she tell Rickie? And how could she get her sister to move on? Olympia smelled the cinnamon, and she actually felt hungry. Maybe something would finally stay down. She resisted stroking her belly, instead propping herself up on the pillows and waiting.

"Here," Rickie said when she came in with the milk and toast.

Olympia focused on the spicy sweetness. This would do it. She took a bite and savored the memories of tucking herself into bed with her sisters, munching toast and giggling. "Perfect."

"Move," Rickie said as she pushed at her sister's legs, so she could sit on the bed. "What's going on? There's dark beer in the fridge, and I checked out what was wrong with the master bedroom. It's obvious a man is living here."

This was why Rickie needed to go to college. The girl was too smart. "You know my daddy left me the house, but there are taxes and repairs. I needed a roommate to make ends meet." Good lie on short notice.

"Then, why are you giving me money?"

"You need it. Plus having a roommate isn't a big deal. And that's all he is." Olympia sipped at the chocolate milk, the coolness soothing her throat and easing her sickness. Could she live on toast, milk and sex?

"Limpy, why are you lying?"

"I'm not lying. I don't mind a roommate. Plus, when I go out on the circuit, it would be good to have someone I can trust here at the ranch."

"Not sure you can call this a ranch." Rickie's nearly turquoise gaze stayed locked on Olympia. Then she shrugged, her lush fall of red hair drifting over her shoulders as she picked at the comforter. "I could get a job, and you could rodeo sooner."

"No," Olympia said flatly. "You need to focus on your schoolwork. I don't mind waiting to get everything in line. I'll be able to go out on some of the amateur rodeos as soon as I find a horse."

"I saw horses when I drove up."

"They're boarders and rescues."

"You look a lot better. You're not white anymore. I'm going to put my stuff in the green room. Where's the air mattress? I can't wait to meet your roommate. I'll bring the horses in while you rest, and then I'll let the sisters know where I am. You all mother-hen me."

Her sister left before Olympia could answer that they mother-henned her because there was something about Rickie that tugged at all of them. Maybe it was her large eyes or soft mouth. They just wanted to protect her from the harsh realities that all the James girls knew firsthand.

Spence wiped his annoyingly sweaty palms on his trousers again as he walked into the ranch house. He had great news, spectacular news. He had been assigned the case in Texas—the big one. Olympia would think she'd gone to heaven, having him out of her hair, right? Except last night had proved once again that they could burn up the sheets.

"Olympia," he shouted as he came into the kitchen through the slider. The house smelled like an actual meal. She must be feeling better. Good, maybe he could convince her to reenact last night. "I've got great news."

"Hey, you must be the roommate," a tall redheaded young woman said as she loped into the kitchen.

"Who the hell are you? And where is my wife?"

"Wife?"

"Yes, wife. Again, who the hell are you?"

"I'm her sister Rickie. What do you mean *wife*? Limpy said that she had a roommate, nothing about getting hitched."

Olympia had told him that she hadn't informed her family about Elvis and the Little Chapel. She said that because they didn't live in visiting distance there was no point in letting them know, especially since they'd be divorced in months. "We got married in Vegas. Love at first sight." Spence allowed his mouth to move while his brain analyzed and filed the information. "I've got to speak with Olympia."

"She's in bed. Why'd you leave her here alone? She's got a bad case of the flu. I found her throwing up—"

Even though he was sure her sickness was the usual, he hurried to see her. He felt for the phone in his pocket in case he needed to call for help.

"Are you okay?" he asked as he opened the door. "Is the baby okay?"

"Baby?" her sister echoed over his shoulder.

"Damn it," Olympia said with feeling.

"You're married and pregnant. What the hell, Limpy?" her sister asked as she pushed past him.

Olympia stared at the two of them. Spence saw the color drain from her face. He spotted the wastebasket and moved to the side of the bed with it. She leaned over and retched.

"It's not the flu, is it, Limpy?" asked Rickie quietly.

Olympia shook her head, lank strands of hair clinging to her face. Spence needed a little time to figure out how this new development affected their situation. He took the wastebasket out to the garbage because he wasn't cleaning that out. He'd get her a new one. Maybe her sister visiting was fate finally giving him a break. He'd worried about leaving her here alone while he went to Texas. He'd tell her he was leaving day after tomorrow and convince her sister to stay and take care of Olympia. It was all good.

He heard their voices as soon as he opened the back door. He knew sibling fighting when he heard it. He and Payson had had similar knockdown fights—literally. "Girls," he said as he went into the bedroom. They turned toward him as one, jaws out and eyes slits of annoyance. "This isn't good for the baby, and I can't afford to replace all our wastebaskets."

"I'm fine, Spence," Olympia said on a huff of breath. She sat up and swung her legs out of the bed. "We'll talk in the kitchen." She stood, closed her eyes for a second and then strode off. She had on shorts that stretched tightly across her butt.

"Perv," her sister accused, clearly noticing the direction of his gaze. "She's pregnant and throwing up. She's not thinking about—"

"I think I know more about how she feels, since I've been—"

"I'm her sister, and I don't believe this baloney about love at first sight."

So Olympia had backed up his story. Good. Much less complicated than trying to explain the prenup.

RICKIE STARED AT the two of them across the sunny-yellow kitchen table, looking skeptical. "You're telling me that you met at Jessie and Payson's wedding, started dating, ran off and got married, and now Limpy's pregnant?"

"Yes," Olympia said with assurance.

Spence decided that he'd keep his lawyer's mouth shut. He didn't really understand the relationship between these two women. He knew something about it from what Olympia had told him at the wedding. She obviously loved her siblings and had sacrificed a lot to make sure they were safe and happy. He could empathize. Not that he'd given up anything for Payson, but for Calvin, he would do whatever he needed to keep the boy out of harm's way.

"So, Spence, is that what you told your brother and your parents?" Rickie asked.

He gathered his thoughts, trying to recall what Olympia had said.

"Time's up. *Eahh!*" Rickie said, making the universal game-show buzzer noise. "If it takes you that long to come up with an answer, you're lying."

"Rickie, stop," Olympia said. "I'm an adult woman. Spence is a good man."

He wondered how much that hurt her to say. Although last night she'd been pretty happy with him. "My brother and sister-in-law know. I don't speak with my parents much."

"That sounds familiar," Rickie said.

"I'll call Mama soon," Olympia answered. "We're happy. It's not exactly how I planned it, but we're good. Right, Spence?" She reached out her hand to grab his, like any couple would do.

He hesitated a moment before clasping hers. It almost felt natural. He gave Olympia a practiced-for-the-jury smile and said, "Better than good. We're doing so well the firm is sending me to Texas on a huge case." The gasp and sudden tension in the room told him that he probably should have worked up to his announcement. How could he be so competent in the courtroom and so lacking in conversational skills at home?

"You're going to Texas? When?" Olympia asked.

At the same time, her sister said, "You're abandoning her while she's so sick and way out here with all these animals?"

"It's just for a week, maybe less, if everything goes well. I'm just a phone call and a flight away."

"Good thing that I'm staying, then, I guess," Rickie said more calmly, looking back and forth between the two of them. What did she see?

"I'll miss you, of course," Olympia obediently added. "But it sounds like a good move for your career." Her lips stretched into a smile; it didn't reach her eyes.

"I know it's sudden, but I wasn't expecting to be the one sent. It must mean that the bosses noticed my work. Plus I'm one of the attorneys licensed to work in Texas, and I can travel on short notice, since I don't have a kid at home."

"Hmm," Rickie said. "So they don't know about the pregnancy?"

"HR does, of course. But I haven't said anything to my bosses. I recently transferred to this office from Phoenix. I want to show them that I'm an asset before I spring the kid on them. Law firms are about billable hours, which babies tend to limit." How the hell was he going to work the billable hours he needed with two children at home? That was a bridge he'd cross later.

"We should celebrate," Olympia said, bracing herself on the table as she stood.

He just stopped himself from putting out a hand to steady her. Rickie was right. It was lucky she'd shown up, because he couldn't have left Olympia here on her own. "I'll help you," he said, following her the few steps to the fridge. He whispered close to her ear, inhaling quickly her Granny Smith–apple scent. "Are you okay? Do you need to lie down?"

"I'm fine," she said, barely moving her lips. "Do you think Rickie's buying our story?"

He looked over his shoulder at his pseudo-sister-in-law. He slid his gaze quickly away from her steady one. "Absolutely," he lied.

"Hope you do better than that in the courtroom."

"What do you mean?"

"That was the worst lie I ever heard." She pulled out a bottle of her prized orange soda. "Here we go. Almost as good as champagne," she said brightly, turning to her sister.

He followed her with glasses and watched as the siblings drank a toast and settled into a conversation about people he didn't know. He once again heard that affection in Olympia's voice. She'd be fine here with Rickie, and he'd made the right decision. Despite what she might say, Olympia cared deeply. If she ever met Calvin, she'd treat him with a warmth that Missy had never been able to achieve.

"You're sleeping in the spare room because of the morning sickness?" he heard Rickie ask. Dang it. The girl wouldn't leave it alone.

"Of course," Olympia said smoothly. "If Spence rolls over in bed, it makes me nauseous, doesn't it, honey?" she asked sweetly.

"For now," he said and meant it. He wanted to share her bed again. He was pretty sure she felt the same way after last night. "I'd say we'd go out to celebrate, but…" he trailed off.

"I'm good with only soup, animal crackers and salsa. No use going out if that's all I can eat."

"That's fine with me. You can help me put the finishing touches on dinner. Help me to get to know my brother-in-law," Rickie said. Spence decided to take her comments at face value.

Olympia hugged her younger sister. "Thanks, Rickie. You always were my favorite."

Rickie's slow smile took her face from pretty to stunning, and right then, he saw the resemblance between these James girls.

"I'm your favorite because I made you cinnamon toast and chocolate milk. Should I try for Grammy's famous eggs with the soup?"

"No," Olympia said in horror, but with a laugh. "Even Spence's stomach couldn't take that."

"What?" he asked, intrigued by the genuine affection and teasing.

"You don't want to know," they said in unison and laughed.

"Come on, cowboy," Rickie said. "Cooking is not just women's work."

He turned to say something to Olympia and was pierced by the look of love that she gave her sister's slowly retreating form. "What?" she asked sharply.

"Nothing. Just happy that someone will be here with you."

"Me, too. I've got to pee." She rushed down the hall, but she definitely wasn't sick. He was nearly certain that he'd seen tears in her eyes. She wasn't the hardened cowgirl she kept telling him she was. With her sister, she was much more like the woman he'd met at the wedding—open, hopeful and funny. Really, Calvin would love her, but his son wouldn't be here anytime soon. Spence's focus had to be on Texas and earning the money for the attorney who would fight for a better custody arrangement. Even if he thought she'd be a good mom figure for Calvin, he didn't want his son getting hurt by thinking that he had a new mom, only to have her abandon him like Missy had.

"Yo, you helping or what?" Rickie asked as she turned to him with a pan of something that smelled great.

"That for me? What are you going to eat?"

"I can take care of myself and my sister," Rickie said, her pretty face firmed into very serious lines. He nodded his head in acknowledgment. These James women were something else.

Olympia missed Spence now that he was in Texas, and she blamed her silliness on her pregnancy hormones. They didn't share a room and barely shared a life. Still, she missed his morning whistling as he got his coffee and his tuneless humming as he ate his generic cereal that was more sugar than nutrition. She shook her head and made the solitary cup of coffee she was allowed to have. She'd sip it and then go out to the barn and forget about Spence, about the baby and about the agreement that made this all temporary.

"I'm going to—"

"Damn it, Rickie. Don't sneak up on me."

"I didn't sneak. You were mooning over that bag of cereal. If you're not going to eat it, give it here." Her sister held out her hand.

What had she been doing with the bag? Imagining Spence eating his breakfast. Pathetic. "Enjoy. I'm going to have yogurt and a banana."

"You couldn't even say that without wrinkling your nose."

"It's healthy and usually stays down."

"I can make you cinnamon toast."

Olympia shook her head, then stopped, not wanting to invite dizziness. "Food is fuel. I've got to get the best fuel into me, like the doctor told me."

"Right, guess that explains your animal-cracker-and-salsa diet."

"That's healthy."

Rickie laughed, low and husky. The sound was so much a part of the younger woman that Olympia had to smile, too. "I think I'll drive into Tucson and see if I can't pick up some work," Rickie said as she put her bowl in the sink. She held up her hand to stop Olympia's protests. "I know it's not long until I start school, but I want to get extra cash coming in. I don't want to freeload."

"I'm happy to have you here. You can help me in the barn. Or better yet, you can clean the house and cook?"

"With the baby and all, I know extra cash would be helpful."

Olympia could see that her sister's mind was made up. She might be generally easygoing, but once Rickie got an idea into her head, there was no way to blast it loose. "I should come with you. The horse boarding isn't exactly paying the bills."

"No way. I know Spence would kick me out if I let you go get a job."

"He's not my keeper."

"Yes, but he's your husband," Rickie said firmly.

Olympia started. Hearing the word *husband* attached

to Spence should make her want to scream, not get warm and mushy. "I'm still my own woman."

"Talk to him about it when he gets back from Texas."

"I don't need to talk with him about it. I'd planned to find another job after our wedding, if I couldn't scare up enough boarders."

"That's between the two of you, and he'll be back in less than a week. Don't get me in the middle of this."

Olympia nodded, letting her sister think it was the threat of Spence's displeasure, not her own queasiness and lack of energy that made getting a job feel impossible. Rickie surprised her with a quick, hard hug.

"Go back to bed until you don't look like death warmed over. I'll be back this afternoon, maybe sooner. Okay?"

"I'm fine."

Rickie shook her head as she left. Olympia felt herself collapsing inward. She was so tired and so sick of being tired and sick. That should be a country-and-western song. She sucked in a deep breath and told herself she just had to see to the horses and then she'd take a nap.

Damn it, her sleep-addled brain said at the sound of pounding. Muffin was using his large hooves to beat on his stall. He'd break the boards if he kept it up. Wait. She was in the house. That was the door. Why was Rickie knocking? Had she gotten locked out? Olympia moved before her brain caught up, pulling open the door to tell her sister off.

"You're not Rickie," Olympia said to the tall blond woman with striking looks, standing on the stoop.

"I'm Missy MacCormack. Who the hell are you?"

"Mommy," a little boy's voice piped up. "That lady's shirt is unbuttoned."

Chapter Seven

Olympia looked down to where a button had popped off—across her getting-bigger-by-the-second honkers. Damn. Darn. She wasn't supposed to swear in front of the kid.

"Where's Spence? I've got to speak with him," the blonde said, her perfectly plucked brows drawn together.

"I'm sorry. He's not here." Olympia's brain slowly perked up. This was the ex. Jeez. The woman was gorgeous, like, on-the-cover-of-*Vogue* beautiful.

"When will he be back?" she asked, clutching at the buttery leather handle of her handbag.

"Mommy, you said Daddy would be here. I want to see Daddy," the little boy said from where he stood plastered against his mother. His pale face, surrounded by wisps of blond hair, reminded her of a tiny bunny peeking out from a nest. His nose even seemed to twitch.

"Spence is in Texas—"

"No," the boy and woman wailed.

"You can call him if you need to speak with him. He might be in court, though."

"You promised," the boy said, his face reddening.

"I didn't know. I'll call him," Missy said, pushing the clinging kid away.

As the woman dialed, the little boy tried to hide behind his mother without touching her. Poor little guy. Olympia had an idea of how scary it was to be dragged into a situation you didn't understand, expecting bad and scary things to happen.

"Pick up, pick up, pick up," Missy breathed into her bejeweled phone. "Payson, as soon as you get this, call me."

Olympia crossed her arms over her chest where the button was missing, very aware of Missy's scornful look.

"This is our son. Calvin." Missy pushed the boy toward her. He kept his head down, his hair sticking out over his ears.

Olympia didn't want to talk to the boy because she didn't want to get involved in whatever this drama was. "Yes. I've seen pictures."

"Spence really lives here?" Missy asked as she looked past Olympia and into the house.

"Crap. Sorry. You wanna come in?" She'd let the implied insult slide since the woman had been stuck standing outside.

"Just a second. Go on, Calvin. Go in. I'll be right back."

The boy hesitated for a second, then scurried into the house. Maybe more mouse than bunny, Olympia thought as she followed him. "Would you like something to drink?" she asked. He shook his head and stopped in the middle of the living room. The broken-down furniture looked worse than usual. "Take a seat," she said. He sidled past her and sat on the edge of the couch. "I'll be back in a minute." She moved quickly down the hall to put on another shirt. She couldn't stand around with her arms crossed.

As she changed, she tried to imagine what Missy could want. Spence and his ex didn't talk, if what he said was true, and he didn't see his son, except in closely supervised visits. "Calvin, you can turn on the TV if you want. I don't know what's—" Olympia stopped when she saw a suitcase and two duffel bags along with a neon-green backpack beside the little boy. His face was whiter than milk, and he looked as if he might throw up. She knew that expression well. "What's this?" she asked gently, determined not to scare him even though her brain screamed *no*.

"My stuff."

"Is there a reason your stuff is here?"

"Yes," he whispered. She took a step closer, and he hugged himself. "Mommy brought it in. She says I have to stay here."

The world went blindingly bright for Olympia as her anger surged. "Your mommy left you here?" She tried to keep her voice soft. She didn't want to terrify the kid any more than he already was. She knew what it was like to be scared because the adults in your life were crazy. Apparently, Missy was certifiable. What mother ditched her kid at someone's house? Well, to be fair, Missy thought of this as Spence's house. But maybe she hadn't left. He might have misunderstood.

Olympia raced to the door and looked out. Nothing. No vehicles, just a distant plume of dust from a car moving fast. She swallowed hard on the nausea that bubbled up. She had to get this settled. *Call Spence.* After all, this was his problem...his kid.

Back inside she said, "I'll call your dad and see what he says. I bet there's some kind of mix-up. You know, like your mom didn't know he was away in Texas. And she'll come back to get you."

"She can't," he said so quietly that Olympia had a tough time hearing him.

"Why not?"

"She's going to rehab. Grandpa Stu and Mimi are mad at her. They yelled, and she said that Daddy should take care of me." His voice hiccuped on a sob.

Olympia wanted to reach out and hug him close, but she reminded herself she wasn't that kind of woman. More important, Spence had agreed that she wouldn't have to be his stepmother. He understood that she wasn't the sort of cowgirl who should be looking after a little boy.

"WHAT ARE YOU going to do?" Rickie whispered to Olympia as the two of them got dinner ready.

"I called Spence and left a message. He'd better have an explanation. Calvin insists that his mom is in rehab, and he's supposed to stay here." Regardless of what Spence said, which better be that he was coming home pronto, Olympia needed to feed Calvin and figure out where he'd sleep. Her current room, she guessed, which meant she had to go back to the master bedroom—which was also a problem. She could handle having another round or two with Spence on the mattress, but she didn't want the intimacy of sharing the space, dividing up the dresser and waking up each morning together. That would make her think all kinds of things that weren't true. Like maybe they were a couple and maybe he was sticking around. None of that would happen. They had a prenup and knew this marriage was ending, sooner rather than later.

"Think how freaked out Calvin must be. I know Mama wasn't much of a parent, but at least she didn't abandon us at other people's houses."

That was about the only thing she hadn't done. "Spence will need to come home and figure it out."

"He's your stepson. You'd eventually have had to deal with him anyway."

"Not right now," Olympia said, slamming her mouth closed on any more words. "This is as good as it's getting." She looked at the stack of sandwiches and the bowl of macaroni salad that Rickie had made with Spam and Velveeta. Comfort food, if Olympia could keep it down. "Go get the kid, and we'll eat." She pulled the phone from her pocket again to check. Nothing from Spence. What the hell…heck. Dam…darn it. Now she had to really watch her language.

"I told Calvin we made our favorite dinner," Rickie said as she herded the little boy to the table. His shoulders were somewhere around his ears. He refused to look anywhere but at the floor. "I also told him that we had root beer to drink, and we could pretend that we were cowboys drinking sarsaparilla."

Calvin shrugged and slunk onto a seat.

Olympia refused to be upset by his mouse-scared movements, which echoed the fears and worries she'd had as a child. "If you don't want root beer, there's milk, iced tea or orange soda."

"I'm not hungry," he whispered.

"You can eat a little of something," Rickie urged, glaring at Olympia, who stood by the table, wanting to keep physical distance between her and the boy. "The salad is the best. We make it only on special occasions. So you being here must be a special occasion."

Calvin didn't lift his head. The defeat in his posture made Olympia's conscience hurt. But she couldn't get sucked into caring about him—or Spence and the baby. Her path was clear.

"What's in it?" the boy mumbled.

"There are secret ingredients," Rickie went on. When had her sister, the youngest, gotten so good with kids? "But it might be awesome macaroni, barrel cactus and a sprinkling of jackrabbit."

The boy's head came up and his blue eyes—the same dusty color as his father's—were wide. "No way."

"Might be. I'm keeping the ingredients secret and those might or might not be what's in it. Give it a taste and tell me."

"I'm a genius, you know. I can figure out when people are fibbing."

"So? I'm going to college, and I know how to make the best macaroni salad in Arizona." Rickie took a big bite and hummed in pleasure. "Best, as always." She looked up at her sister and motioned with her head for her to sit.

Olympia couldn't move. She couldn't be part of this. She didn't want Calvin to get the idea that he was staying or that Olympia was anything like a stepmom. "Um, I've... I... There. Don't you hear that? It's Muffin. He needs me to, um, check on him." She moved to the patio slider to escape from the kitchen to the barn or maybe take the car and race away.

"If you say so, Limpy, but come right back and have supper because—"

"Sure," she said and was outside, gulping in the hot,

dry air. She didn't stop until she was in the barn, the cool darkness giving her a chance to assure herself that she really could finish out this marriage, hand over the baby and then go be in the rodeo. That was her route to happiness; nothing would move her from it, not Calvin and certainly not Spence. And definitely not the peanut of a baby.

Since she was in the barn anyway, she may as well check on the animals. She was a cowgirl, and that was what a cowgirl did.

Hours later in the dark bedroom that had become Spence's and was now hers again, Olympia lay awake, waiting for his call and hoping her danged husband had an easy solution for getting his son out of the house quickly. Rickie couldn't help because she believed it was a real marriage. She said she'd cut Olympia some slack about hiding in the barn since she was pregnant— which they weren't telling Calvin. Then Rickie had gone out to meet friends for a fun night out. Something that had never been on Olympia's to-do list because she was saving money or watching her siblings. How had she gone from being an independent, nearly-to-the-rodeo woman back to taking care of her sister and a kid? That one night with Spence. She was going to be paying for that for a long time.

Her phone rang. She hesitated, feeling vulnerable and slightly weepy here in the dark—not the way she wanted to confront attorney Spencer MacCormack, aka Liar, Liar Pants on Fire. She picked up the phone anyway, sitting up in bed and turning on the light. "Finally," she said.

"Hello to you, too. I've been busting my butt here.

I couldn't call earlier. They're not paying me to check in with my wife."

"I would have sent you a text, but that didn't seem right—"

"What's happened? Are you at the hospital?"

His tone was sharp, reminding her that he cared about her only as the incubator for his baby and maybe as the wild cowgirl in his bed. "No. This is your mess and it's lucky the doctor has me on those antinausea pills, otherwise today would have turned my stomach inside out. Missy stopped by—"

"I saw that she called—"

"Stop interrupting and I'll tell you." She waited a moment and then went on, "Missy stopped by today and dropped off Calvin. Actually, she just left him—"

"Calvin is at the ranch? Did she not understand her parents' visitation schedule?"

"She's going to rehab and wants you to take care of Calvin. I found paperwork in his backpack. Apparently, it was a condition she set for returning to rehab."

"I… What…? Calvin's at the house right now?"

"He's asleep."

"What else did Missy say?"

"Nothing. I left the room for a couple of minutes. When I came back, there was a pile of Calvin's stuff and Missy was gone."

"Damn it. Why? I can't—"

"You've got to come home. You promised that I wouldn't have to—"

"Hell. I can't leave. If I leave, I'll lose my job. Then, where will we all be? I should be done in three days, maybe four. I'll try Jessie, see if she can come down and help. Calvin knows her, but she's so busy."

Olympia knew he was right about work. And Jessic was up to her eyeballs right now. She'd taken on setting up another program in California, commuting a couple times a week. Damn...darn! "This is an emergency. There have to be rules about emergencies."

"It would be an emergency if my wife wasn't at home to look after my son."

Crap. "I could call her parents to come and get him."

"If you do, what will they think? That you don't want Calvin, which will make my petition seem odd, since my 'loving wife' doesn't want anything to do with her stepson."

"Well, your 'loving wife' doesn't. You said Calvin would never be here, that I would need to be a stepmom in name only." She felt tears of frustration gathering. Da...darn these hormones. She would not cry.

"Look, I can't leave. I might be able to swing a day early, but that's still at least two more days." She heard him draw in a deep breath. "Please. He's just a little boy. He didn't ask for any of this. I know that you can do it. You raised your sisters—"

"Which is exactly why I didn't want Calvin here," she said, her voice rising. *Get a grip*, she told herself firmly. "Don't you know anyone else?"

"Olympia, if you don't do this for me, then I'll consider you in breach of our prenup and subsequent contract, which will forfeit any moneys promised to you. I may even have a case for a suit, and I know a good lawyer." His voice had steel and maybe a hint of desperation.

"What the hell? You wouldn't... You couldn't... You..." She sputtered to a halt, stiffening her spine and clutching at the phone. "That's blackmail."

"No, it's a good agreement, which I'll remind you again that I told you to have your own attorney look at."

"Shut up, you stupid ass," Olympia yelled into the phone. She could not be responsible for his son. It would be too easy to—

"You said a bad word," Calvin accused, peering through the door.

"Shi…sheets," she said with feeling.

"What?" Spence asked through the phone.

Her gaze remained locked on the kid as she put the phone down. "Hey, sorry I was a little loud."

"Daddy says no swears."

"I'm sure he does, but he's not here…" Her voice trailed off as the soft light in the room glistened on the tracks of tears on his cheeks. "He's on the phone. Do you want to talk with him?"

"Is he coming to get me?"

Her throat closed with remembered fears, but she sucked it up and answered, "He's in Texas. Here." She held out the phone and was proud that she wasn't trembling. Spence could deal with this, she assured herself. He was the dad. That was his job, not that she had much experience with parenthood. Calvin crept farther into the room and snatched the phone from the bed, turning his back to her.

"Daddy?" His thin voice wavered. A moment of silence, and his hunched shoulders relaxed. "I woke up, and that lady wasn't here. I couldn't find her." More silence. "Not *her*," he said with a quick glance over his shoulder.

Yeah, well, I feel the same way. So he liked Rickie better than her.

"Daddy wants to talk to you." Calvin stood as far away as he could, holding out the phone to her.

This would not be pleasant. "What?" she asked Spence.

"He's scared. My God, he's a little boy. Would it kill you to show him some empathy?"

It might, that dark part of her mind said. The part that would protect her at any cost, that had protected her and her sisters from a mother probably not too different from Missy.

"Fine. Be a—" She heard him stop the word. "This isn't what any of us want, but you're the adult. It's for just a few days."

Calvin stood halfway to the door. He looked ready to run if he had to. Dear Lord. What was wrong with her? A little boy was terrified of her. She didn't want to be chummy, but she didn't need to scare the piss out of him. Was she more like her mother than she allowed herself to think?

"Olympia?"

"Sure. A few days. We can make it through a few days. He can help exercise the horses and clean out the barn."

"Absolutely not," Spence said at the same time that Calvin's blue gaze locked on to hers, both hopeful and excited. "He's still recovering from surgery. It's much too dangerous for him—"

"He's got to do something in the afternoons. He can't sit in the house."

She hadn't noticed that the boy had crept closer, until he whispered, "Horses. You have horses."

She nodded and had to ask Spence to repeat what he'd said. The hopeful note in Calvin's tone made her feel…well, less like an evil hag and more like Glinda the Good Witch.

"He's not to go in the barn. The hay could trigger breathing problems, and your animals are dangerous. Calvin has tested into the ninety-fifth percentile. He can entertain himself on his tablet, or take him to the library for books."

"Library? He should be outdoors." Calvin looked at her with resignation and just a hint of interest.

"Calvin missed a lot of instruction with his illness and surgeries. If he'd been with me, he'd be going to summer school to catch up. In fact, I'll see if there are some nearby summer camps that he could attend."

"Maybe he'd like the same rodeo camp that Jessie and I went to? I think they're still in business." Calvin's skinny little body quivered with excitement, and then Olympia felt bad. There was no way Spence would let him go, and she knew it. She shouldn't have used him to get back at his dad. God. She really was bad at this.

"Don't tell him that. He is not going to a rodeo camp. Let me do research. Damn. I've got to go. I'm getting a text. I'll call tomorrow morning with a solution."

She tried to say something but he'd already hung up. "So…" Olympia wasn't sure what else to say.

"I can see the horses tomorrow. Promise?"

She looked at his dusty blue eyes and just couldn't say no. "Why not? No riding, though." She saw him lose a little enthusiasm. "Time to get back in bed." The boy immediately stiffened.

"Maybe I could watch TV?"

"It's late. You need to be in bed." She got up and started pushing him out the door. After he was asleep, she'd figure out how this was going to work.

Outside his bedroom, he stopped and whirled to her, "It's really dark in there, and the closet door—" He sucked in a breath and went on, "It closed all by itself."

Shi…sheets. The house was so out of plumb that the door often did that. She'd forgotten, but she could remember childhood well enough to know she'd have totally freaked out, too. "It's just that the house isn't built that well," she said, and walked across the room to flip the light switch behind the dresser mirror. She heard him heave out another breath. He'd woken scared and then couldn't even find the light. She didn't look at him, because if she did, she might feel even worse. "See?" She opened up the closet. "Nothing in here."

"Does it have a trapdoor?"

"A trapdoor?"

"Into the attic, because then somebody could get on the roof, kick in that little window up there and come down through the trapdoor."

"No. There's one in the kitchen closet." His eyes got huge. Wrong answer. "But…I nailed it shut so no one can get in through there."

"How many nails?"

"A dozen." He looked skeptical. "Big nails."

"Do you have a cat?"

"No. Why would you think I have a cat?"

"I don't know. I was just checking."

"No more stalling. Into bed," Olympia said. Her sisters had had similar routines to try to stay up late.

Calvin hesitated and then slid under the covers, his eyes darting around the room. She saw him gaze longingly at a creature she'd never seen before and might have been a stuffed animal somewhere in its past.

"Do you want—?" She picked up the lump and gestured to him. He shook his head, but his eyes never left it. "I'll just put it on the nightstand, so no one steps on it and breaks an ankle. Want me to leave the light on?"

"No," he said, his voice shaking a little.

"Okay. I'll leave a light on in the hall so you can find your way to the bathroom." He relaxed a fraction. She turned off the light. At the bedroom door, she stopped and pulled it partway closed. "Is that enough light?"

"A little more closed."

"Okay?"

"No, no, too much."

She opened it farther. "Now?" It took nearly five minutes before he was satisfied by the amount of light coming in the room. Finally, she said, "Good night."

She went back to the master bedroom. What was she going to do with a kid around here? She'd talk Rickie into watching him. Her sister had an easy way about her, and she hadn't gotten a job yet. She could look out for the boy. That relaxed Olympia marginally, except Rickie hadn't come home yet. Her sister was young and responsible, but still there was a lot of trouble she could get into. And then there were their genes. Olympia was thinking about Rickie meeting up with a fast-talking cowboy and couldn't fall asleep for another hour.

Chapter Eight

Olympia knew she looked like...heck, which was just great because she had a potential boarder coming, and, of course, there was her stepson, who'd already told her that he didn't eat cereal, toast or eggs for breakfast. He ate only waffles with blueberry syrup. When she'd told him that wasn't happening, he'd raced back to his room and slammed the door. Then Rickie had come stumbling down the hall, given Olympia the evil eye and locked herself in the bathroom.

Olympia's rest had been broken by either sexy dreams of Spence or the urge to pee—they were both annoying. Just as she'd fallen into a deep sleep, the alarm had gone off. Now she was trying to get by on her one cup of coffee. She had the barn to clean, potential clients to impress and a stepson underfoot. That surely needed more than one cup of caffeine, but the doctor had told her Peanut couldn't take the stimulation.

The client had come and gone. No new horses to board. The ranch was too far away, and Muffin had decided today was the day that he'd act like a rabid animal. He hammered on the walls with his hooves and bugled out his displeasure at who knew what. She'd come back in the house to feel as if she was doing something useful and search sites for potential new boarders. She'd been at it for an hour or more when her stomach did a flip, telling her it was time for lunch—for her and for Calvin. Rickie could fend for herself. Although her sister may have left. She'd thought she'd heard a car, but she'd been so focused on the screen that she wasn't sure.

"Calvin…Cal," she called, walking into the living room.

She heard a faint noise coming from the master bedroom. What was the boy doing in there? Something he shouldn't, probably. She tiptoed as quietly as her boots allowed on the tiled hallway and pushed the door open. Cal whipped around from where he sat in the middle of the bed. His stuffed animals, scattered over the messy sheets, looked innocent enough. But Cal's red ears told her another story.

"Why are you in here?" she blurted.

"Just playing." He dropped his head, and his shoulders nearly reached his ears.

"What's wrong with your room?"

He shrugged.

It couldn't still be the scary closet. It was daylight. "What do you want for lunch?"

He shrugged again, not looking at her and fiddling with the dirty, lumpy "animal" that he'd insisted last night wasn't anything he wanted.

"I'll call you when it's ready." He kept quiet and stared at the small collection of toys. She went to the kitchen and opened the fridge, but nothing appealed to her. She wanted fry bread with beans and cheese with salsa verde from Rita's. Rickie's car was gone, but Spence's keys were here. He'd left the vehicle for her to use because her truck, which he'd taken to the airport, was a "death trap." She trudged back to the bedroom, stopping when she heard Cal talking.

"Okay, troops. We have to stick together. Daddy won't be home for a while, and we've got to stay with some lady. Daddy said we have to listen, but we don't 'cause she's not our mom. She'll never be our mom. Mommy is at rehab. When she comes home, she and Daddy will get back together, and *she'll* be out on her... her...derriere."

Damn...dang it, Olympia said to herself, tears in her eyes. She should feel insulted, but instead she felt bad for the little boy. He wanted what every other kid wanted, what she'd wanted so badly when she was little: a mom and dad living together and making a nice home. Well, she'd survived without it, and she was all right. He'd be fine, too. Plus, his mom was no prize. The jury was still out on his dad.

"Hey," she said softly to Cal when it seemed as if there was a break in his speech.

He turned to her, his wispy hair flying and his eyes blazing with annoyance. "Stop snooping."

"I wasn't snooping." *Liar.* "I just wanted to tell you that we're going out for lunch at—"

"I'm not going."

"You can't stay here, and I'm hungry for fry bread." Bribing her sisters with food had sometimes worked. Rickie had been willing to do almost anything for a Cansito snack cake with the nasty strawberry filling.

"There's food here. I'll eat that."

"When we get back, you can come out to the barn and feed the horses their treats," she wheedled. She really wanted fry bread, and she couldn't leave Cal here on his own, could she? No. She could not. He was only seven.

"And I get to ride."

He was his father's son—trying to negotiate for more. "Treats today and tomorrow."

"Just sitting on a horse, then." His gaze locked on her, filled with hope.

How could she say no to that? "Okay. Five minutes."

"And a walk around the corral."

"Don't push it, kid."

He nodded, his smile breaking out with the dimple that was just like his father's. She could see what a handsome man he'd become, despite his current scrawny paleness. Tears sprang to her eyes again. Dang hormones.

PASQUALE LOOKED AS enthused waiting for his passenger as Olympia felt. She heard the scuff of pebbles that must be Cal. She'd sent him back in the house to change from shorts and a T-shirt into jeans, a long-sleeved shirt and a bike helmet that she'd seen in his closet. It wasn't as good as a riding helmet, but it was better than nothing. He had to wear sneakers because he didn't have boots. What boy who lived in Arizona didn't have boots? His daddy had boots, even if they weren't workingman's boots. Olympia would need to get him a real helmet and boots. No. He wasn't staying. No use in investing in those.

"What's wrong with him?" Cal pointed at Pasquale, whose nearly closed eyes and cocked foot made it clear that he'd rather be napping. This rescue horse had *the* most laid-back attitude. It sort of matched his hide, neither brown nor gray but some color in between that always looked as if he'd just rolled in dirt. Although rolling in dirt would probably be too much work for Pasquale. She'd been told that he might be part sloth when she'd agreed to foster him.

"Pasquale's into energy conservation." She pulled on the cinch. The gelding opened his eyes a smidgen more and tried to inflate his lungs so she wouldn't be able to get the cinch as tight as she needed to hold the saddle securely in place. A trick horses learned early on. "No way," she said, pulling harder on the strap, lifting her knee and pushing it against his side. That was enough to remind the horse. He sighed heavily, and she made a final adjustment. "You ready?"

The boy nodded but didn't move. "He's pretty big."

"Not that big." Pasquale wasn't a pony, but most people wouldn't consider him horse-size, either. "Put your foot in here," Olympia said, making a cradle for his foot to give him the boost that he'd need to get in the saddle. No foot landed in her hands. She looked at the boy through her eyelashes. He trembled a little, his face paler than usual. "You don't have to do this."

"You promised."

"It's up to you, but if you're scared—"

"I'm not scared."

Olympia stood. A fine tremor ran through Cal. The kid was obviously afraid and didn't want to let her know. She ached as she watched him fight his fear. When Olympia visited Hope's Ride, what had Jessie said to the kids in her program if they worried about getting on a horse? "Pasquale knows when I put the saddle on him that it's time for a rider to get on his back. It's his very favorite thing, and he won't do anything to knock you off because he wants to be able to have you sit on him again."

"Are you fibbing?"

"Pasquale, am I fibbing?" she asked the horse, pulling just a little on his reins. He naturally pulled his head up and down against the tension.

Cal smiled, showing off the familiar dimple. She bent over, ignoring that little tug the similarity to his father gave her. "Put your foot here," she said, making her hands once again into a cradle. She easily boosted him up. They stood in the corral, Cal stiff as a board as Pasquale went back to dozing. What could happen if she led Cal around? It'd make him happy, and Pasquale could use the exercise. The horse's ears swiveled as she tugged lightly on the halter. He snuffled the air and went into his plodding walk.

"I'm riding," Cal said, and the smile did not leave his face for the next twenty minutes as she led the horse around the corral.

"Okay. Now you take him around." His eyes got big as his skinny little fingers tightened on the reins. "You'll do fine." She patted Cal's leg, gentling him like she would a skittish horse. "I will be right here." She saw him firm his boyishly soft chin.

The horse snorted, and Cal's body tensed. "He just got dust in his nose. He's fine. Remember, he likes to have a rider on his back. He won't do anything that will mean he can't have you ride him again."

She stood in the center of the small corral. If she had to race to help him, she could. He didn't have much form, sitting stiffly and not rocking with the motion of the horse, but his genuine grin made her feel good. He might not have the problems that the kids in Jessie's therapeutic-riding program had, but Olympia'd bet that he'd get similar benefits from working with the horses. She'd treat him like a student, not her stepson. Supportive but with a little distance. She could do that.

"I want to go faster. How do I make him go faster?" Cal's little boy voice piped up and over the corral. She caught the frantic drumming of his heels against Pasquale's side. The horse threw his head in annoyance and sped up a little, making Cal bounce. She hurried to him, grabbing the horse's head.

"You're not ready yet. You need to practice the walk first, then you can go faster."

"I want to go now."

"No. Pasquale's tired." She tugged again on the rein, and the horse nodded his head. She saw the disappointment on Cal's face, but he didn't protest. After she got him down and got him to help her care for the horse, he stayed in the barn, asking questions and fetching things she needed.

Olympia looked over at Cal's earnest face as he watched her working the other horses using a longe line—the long rein that allowed her to stand in the middle of the corral while the horses went through their paces in a circle around her. The doctor had nixed riding at her first appointment, so this was the only way for her to exercise the animals—including the cranky Muffin.

By the time supper rolled around, both Olympia and Cal were tired. She put together sandwiches so they could eat in front of the TV. Meanwhile, Rickie, who had a better social life than one of those teen stars on TMZ, was out again.

Olympia woke with Cal leaning against her on the couch; some rodeo rerun was on the TV. She needed to pee badly...as usual. Cal had his thumb in his mouth. Her throat tightened at the innocence of him, the loveliness of the promise of his future in the miniature face. She tried to pick him up, but though small for his age, she couldn't do it. Instead, she got him to his feet, letting him lean heavily on her, his warm weight anchoring her to the world in the middle of the night. It made the growing Peanut inside her seem less like an alien and more like a miracle.

She shook her head as she got him under the covers. She went to her own room, put on Spence's shirt and crawled into bed, reminding herself that the miracle would be someone else's—Spence's and the woman he married for real. He was the kind of man meant to have a wife and family.

She rolled onto her side, pulling up her knees to soothe the ache in her back. How was she going to make it through months more of the sickness—which still struck at odd times—and the backaches? She'd do it, just like she'd made sure her sisters got fed even when she had to use a stool to cook on the stove. You did what it took to survive.

Spence had been sitting in his Texas hotel for hours, plowing through material so he could get home sooner rather than later. He'd already stayed three more days than he'd anticipated. His phone started vibrating on the table serving as his desk. Olympia. He'd already spoken with Calvin. Now Olympia was calling? He'd let voice mail get it. The phone stopped vibrating. He pushed around the food on his plate. After a moment, the phone vibrated again.

"Yes," he barked.

"I, um, I wanted to make sure that Cal called you."

"Hours ago."

"Good."

"Did you want something else? I've still got work to get done."

"No. Well…yes."

Silence. Then she said, "I'm sorry, but it's not working out."

His lungs stopped moving. "Excuse me?"

"I've tried. I mean really tried, but…I don't know what to say… How to…"

Spence heard tears as her voice trailed off. What the…? Was she going to break the agreement? Walk out on him? On Calvin? A wall of fear and desolation crashed down on him. "We can talk when I get home. This isn't something that we can settle on the phone. I won't be here much longer."

"Da…dang hormones," Olympia sniffled. "I just can't…" Her words melted into a wet-sounding stream of nonsense.

"Don't do anything until I get there." A new fear lodged in his throat. What if she followed through on her threat to run away? His brain went into overdrive. Could he get a flight from Texas and talk some sense into her before his bosses and client realized that he was gone?

"What? Why are you going to come home?" she asked her voice sharper.

"To stop you."

"Stop me? From what? I'm not going to kill Jessie." That sounded like *his* Olympia, then her voice quavered. "She made her sister—Lavonda—come and help me because she couldn't. Now Lavonda's taking over. Muf-

fin listens to her, even if she doesn't have a muffin…"
Olympia's voice broke again. "I know it's stupid, but she
left ranching and I'm the one who is making a career of
it and she's better at this than me and it's not fair that—"

"You're jealous of Lavonda?" he asked, relief making him giddy as blood rushed to his head from where
it had hardened into a cold lump in his throat.

"Don't laugh at me."

"I'm not laughing." At that moment, his brain short-
circuited and a loud bark of laughter burst from him.

"You are, too."

"Am not."

"Are, too." She chortled, clear and easy. His shoulders loosened. "What are we? Six years old? Sorry. I'm
being silly and hormonal."

He got up and walked to the bed. She went on talking about things at the ranch. The normal small talk any
couple had, and he found himself enjoying it. Except
they weren't a couple.

"It's getting late. Guess I'd better go," she finally
said.

"Dawn does come early. Before you hang up, how
are you feeling? No nausea? Have you gone shopping?"

"I'm fine. The pills are working. I told you I don't
need anything."

"You were busting out of everything. You're more
than four months pregnant. You shouldn't ask your
clothing to make such sacrifices. I bet you're wearing
that Mickey Mouse T-shirt."

"Maybe."

"I knew it. Honestly, Olympia, we can afford new
clothes. You can't ignore the baby."

"No way to do that."

"I know this is all new to you—"

"It's not. I remember Mama pregnant. I have no idea how I kept my sisters from getting pregnant, but they didn't, even when it seemed as though every one of their friends was getting knocked up."

He heard the anger, the fear and something else he couldn't name. "Have you felt the baby move yet?" he asked cautiously.

"Not yet," she said quietly.

"Then, you should get all the sleep you can now. That'll help your dark circles."

"Those are gone."

"Then, you're getting that glow."

"That's sunburn."

He laughed. They were once again back to the easy banter. He'd missed having another adult to talk to the past few years as he'd worried about Calvin and negotiated with Missy and her family. "Really. I bet you look good. Let me buy you new things to show off that belly of yours."

"You mean my breasts, don't you? They're enormous."

The air seemed to disappear from the room as he saw in his mind the way her chest had pressed against the fabric of even her largest shirts—and he'd always thought he was a leg man. "They're beautiful," he breathed.

He barely heard her next words. "They ache all the time."

He hesitated for a moment before saying, "When I get home, I'll massage them until you... That'll make them feel better." He stopped himself from saying more because he wanted to do this and more to make her feel good. There might have been a part of him that needed to make her feel better and maybe a little sexy, too—darn it. "I've got to go. Just got a text," he lied, turning off the phone before he said something really stupid to his pretend wife.

OLYMPIA CURLED UP in her bed, wearing one of Spence's shirts, staring at the silent phone. She'd taken to sleeping in it because she didn't have any nightgowns. Yep. That was exactly why she'd worn it.

She even—darn her stupid hormones—wanted to snuggle into bed and relive those flashes of sexy heat she'd heard in his voice. But she couldn't. She and Spence weren't a couple, not really. She had to remember that. While her desire for him fought with her nausea, it was just another physical need, like all those other ones. Her body had taken on a life of its own—literally—so all kinds of things were happening to her that she didn't want or agree with. Like her breasts. She'd have to start wearing a sports bra to keep everything in place and dig into the back of her closet for bigger, baggier pants. Her mama always bragged that she'd never needed maternity clothes, not that Olympia wanted to be like her mama. But here she was, pregnant after one night. Maybe this was different because she and Spence were actually married, even if it was just on paper.

Their marriage might end sooner than planned since Cal was already living with them, though. She'd ended up keeping her distance by viewing the little boy like one of the rescue horses who were just passing through. That meant not getting too attached and making just as sure the horse—or the little boy—didn't think it was anything more.

More important, unlike her mama, when her "man" left, he'd be taking the baby with him. It was right there in the contract. In black, white and a ton of subsections. Cal would forget her, like the horses did and just the way she had all her "daddies." The baby would never know her—which was for the best. No one wanted someone like her as their mom.

A glass of milk. That was what she needed right now. Pregnant women needed milk, she'd read that somewhere. But when she got to the kitchen, milk no longer appealed to her. She stared into the fridge, gave up and wandered into the living room. Turning on the TV would wake Cal and Rickie—if her sister was even home. Maybe she should say something to her about the late nights. No, Rickie had her head on straight.

Why couldn't she settle? When the alarm went off tomorrow morning, she'd be exhausted, so why wasn't she going to bed? The little voice that she regularly ignored said, *Because you don't want to be in that bed all alone.*

Chapter Nine

Spence's stomach growled, but he ignored it. He felt that indefinable urge to get home to the ranch. He'd spoken to his son two days ago and exchanged a number of texts. Olympia had been increasingly silent as his time in Texas had stretched into nearly a month. He didn't expect her to chitchat, but her clipped tone worried him. He feared that he'd come home and only Rickie and Calvin would be there. In his more rational moments, he knew his worries had more to do with the way his ex had been than the way Olympia was acting.

More than one evening, he'd come home to baby Calvin sleeping in his crib and no Missy. She'd been out with friends or in a nearby apartment having "just one drink," which always turned into an entire evening of partying. It was dangerous behavior, no matter what, but with a baby like Calvin, who'd had his own monitor because of his heart problems, it could have been deadly.

He hit Dial on his phone and listened to the rings. Why weren't they picking up? He pushed a little harder on the accelerator, passing a nondescript gray car. Less than a minute later, he caught the flashing lights in the rearview mirror. Damn it. He pulled to the side of the road, thinking that he'd give Olympia a piece of his mind when he saw her for not picking up the phone. If she'd done that, he wouldn't have been speeding.

One hour and a five-hundred-dollar ticket later, Spence opened up the throttle on Olympia's truck as he pushed it over the last hill to the ranch—he hoped the spurt of speed would relieve his annoyance.

The ranch house and buildings looked deserted, no horses in the corral and the house shut up tight. Where was everyone? Why was the day so blasted hot and why was he wearing a suit? He pulled off his jacket and yanked open the top buttons on his shirt before he strode through the back door. The patio was blessedly cool and dark but too quiet. He walked toward the barn. What was Olympia thinking, having his son out in this heat? Calvin's operation had repaired his damaged heart, but he needed to be careful. He was fragile. Spence's purposeful stride sped up to a run. Where were they? What was wrong? The dread he'd felt driving him from Texas ratcheted up another three notches.

"Let me, let me."

He heard his son's voice come drifting from the barn. He didn't wait for his eyes to adjust to the dimness.

"Watch out," Olympia said as there was a clink of metal on metal and a horsey snort.

Spence ran now, his lungs burning.

"Make him stop." Calvin's shrill voice pierced Spence's heart. More snorts and a low, firm "whoa." He got to the stall, his chest so tight with fear he couldn't take a full breath. He put out his hand to open the half door.

"Look, Dad," Calvin said, his voice excited. "Pasquale likes me. He lets me brush him. He was all dirty. He rolled in poop. It was kind of gross, but Olympia said that a cowboy has to take care of his mount."

"Your mount?" Spence panted and stared death rays at Olympia. He'd told her and she'd promised that, no matter what, Calvin would not get on a horse. How had his son kept it a secret from him during their calls?

"He's done well, Spence," Olympia said in a soothing voice he figured she used on recalcitrant horses.

"I don't care. You promised—"

"Dad," Calvin interrupted. "I wear a helmet and everything. It's totally safe, and we never go anywhere but the corral, and Pasquale—"

"You're not strong enough," Spence said and knew he'd uttered the words sure to make his son go from pleasant to raging.

"I am, too. You always say that, and you're wrong." Calvin clamped his lips into a frown and put his hands on his hips.

"I know you're strong, son, but horses are different. They're unpredictable. Look at Aunt Jessie. She's fallen off more than one horse and hurt herself." Spence reached over the half door to pull Calvin toward him. The sleepy-looking horse perked up, snorted and grabbed Spence's arm between its yellow teeth. He tried to pull away, but the horse hung on.

"Pasquale," Olympia said, reaching out and grabbing the horse's halter.

"Stop, Olympia," Spence said as the horse clamped down tighter.

She stood stock-still for a second, indecision written large on her face, then Calvin moved to the horse's mouth and pulled it open. "Bad, Pasquale," he said. "Don't bite my dad. That's mean."

The horse immediately let go and stepped back. Spence was sure that his horsey gaze said, *Watch it, buddy. Next time I take a finger.* Spence wasn't even certain what had set the animal off. "Calvin, come out of there. Obviously that horse has an attitude problem."

"They've really bonded," Olympia said.

His son added, "Me and Pasquale are buddies. He's real gentle and lets me pet him all the time, even without treats."

Spence closed his eyes, not feeling any less stressed. His fragile son thought this huge animal was safe. Worse, he was falling in love with it. Wouldn't that be great when Spence had to tear him away from Pasquale?

"Come on, Cal-boy, time to let Pasquale nap," Olympia said. "You know he's part sloth and has got to get his sixteen hours of sleep a day or he's cranky." Calvin giggled as he and Olympia came out of the stall.

Spence looked at both of them, his small-for-his-age son and his "wife" and mother of his new child. He wanted to knock sense into both of them for scaring him.

"Don't worry so much, Dad. I'm real strong now. Look at my muscles." Calvin showed off his scrawny biceps. "Remember, the doctor said I was all fixed."

For now he was fixed, Spence thought, but what if something happened?

"We're done out here," Olympia said into the silence. "You want a snack, Cal?"

"His name is Calvin," Spence said, and the two of them glared at him. "Well, it is."

"It's a stupid name," Calvin muttered.

"It's your great-great-grandfather's."

"Don't care."

Spence had never thought his son didn't like the name. He'd been so proud to carry on the family tradition. His son's namesake had been a lawman in Texas and New Mexico before settling in Arizona.

"Snack time," Olympia said. "You're cranky because your blood sugar is low." She pushed his son in front of her. It wasn't just her body that seemed softer, more womanly. Even her voice had taken on a gentler tone. Spence watched the two of them leave the barn, thinking that the sight made him simultaneously sentimental and suspicious of his own happiness. Forget the horse. How had Calvin bonded with Olympia? He'd wanted her to treat Calvin well, but he didn't think a relationship was a good idea. What would happen when they inevitably split up? It would be bad.

When Spence got into the house, Calvin and Olympia were at the kitchen counter, fixing a snack and drink...and laughing. What was he going to do? He had to protect his son. The original plan had been that once he got full custody of Calvin and the baby was born, he'd move out and move on. Olympia had sworn she was taking care of the boy but holding him at arm's length. He wasn't so sure. He needed to make changes now, separate his son more from her, help him create distance.

"Limpy, Rickie and me are going to the Dairy Queen. You wanna come, Dad?"

"Limpy?" he asked his son sternly.

Olympia looked up from the plate of salsa she was shoveling into her mouth with animal crackers. "What's the big deal?"

"'Limpy' is disrespectful." God, he sounded like one of those stuffy judges he'd encountered in small-town courts.

Olympia shrugged. "Are you coming?"

"What about dinner?"

"That's hours away. We won't spoil our appetites. Will we, Cal-boy? Get it? 'Cause it sounds like cowboy." She turned to his son with a grin. "We've been working hard all morning and afternoon. It's time for a real treat. Rickie," she yelled as she stood.

"Limpy's pregnant. I looked that up after you told me. She's got the cravings and everything."

Spence felt himself blush. He'd put her pregnancy at the back of his mind, even the changes he'd noticed when he'd first seen her. He moved restlessly.

"Calvin can have a treat after dinner. There's a freezer full of them."

"Yuck," his usually biddable son said, sticking out his tongue. "Those are healthy, and we don't want healthy."

"Did you teach him that?" he glared at Olympia, who didn't look guilty.

"They are healthy, not gooey and sugary, like a double-chocolate mudslide with extra caramel and brownie chunks."

"Yeah, Dad."

"Yeah, Dad," Rickie echoed as she strolled down the hall. "Dairy Queen rules. Frozen yogurt drools."

Spence looked at the trio and put on his in-command-of-the-jury face. "We can go after dinner. First, Calvin, you need to show me how you spent all your time while I was away. I know you had that puzzle and the LEGO Millennium Falcon I ordered for you." He guided his son down the hall toward his bedroom. Spence told himself that he wasn't petty enough to be annoyed that his son hadn't been as excited to see him as he'd been imagining on the drive to the ranch.

"Why don't you like Limpy? You're married and everything," Calvin said. "Are you going to get divorced like you and Mommy?"

Crap. "Grown-ups—"

"I asked Limpy, and she said that every marriage is different, like there are all kinds of M&M's. She said you guys are like candy-corn M&M's because they aren't for everyone and aren't around all the time, but they're still M&M's."

Spence had no idea what M&M's had to do with marriage, but obviously Olympia and his son had talked about it. What else had she said? This was exactly what he didn't want to happen. "You don't need to worry. You know I love you and that I always do what's best for you."

"I like it here. I like Pasquale."

"After the baby, you know that Olympia plans to go on the road with the rodeo. She won't even be living here."

"She'd never sell the ranch," Calvin said with a lot more vehemence than Spence expected. "She won't be gone all the time, and Pasquale and Muffin will have to have a place to live."

Dear Lord, Spence had to break up his son and Olympia right now. He didn't want Calvin hurt by another woman, like he'd been by Missy. "That's months from now. A lot can change."

"Yeah, like there will be a baby around here."

"You're right. Now show me what you've been up to." Spence redirected his son because his big old lawyer's brain hadn't come up with a good way to explain the situation to Calvin.

Send For
2 FREE BOOKS
Today!

I accept your offer!

Please send me two
free novels and two mystery
gifts (gifts worth about $10).
I understand that these books
are completely free—even
the shipping and handling will
be paid—and I am under no
obligation to purchase anything,
ever, as explained on the back
of this card.

154/354 HDL GJAE

Please Print

FIRST NAME

LAST NAME

ADDRESS

APT.#   CITY

STATE/PROV.   ZIP/POSTAL CODE

Visit us online at
www.ReaderService.com

Offer limited to one per household and not applicable to series that subscriber is currently receiving.
Your Privacy—The Reader Service is committed to protecting your privacy. Our Privacy Policy is available
online at www.ReaderService.com or upon request from the Reader Service. We make a portion of our mailing
list available to reputable third parties that offer products we believe may interest you. If you prefer that we not
exchange your name with third parties, or if you wish to clarify or modify your communication preferences, please
visit us at www.ReaderService.com/consumerchoice or write to us at Reader Service Preference Service, P.O. Box
9062, Buffalo, NY 14240-9062. Include your complete name and address.

AR-815-GF15

© 2015 HARLEQUIN ENTERPRISES LIMITED. ® and ™ are trademarks owned and used by the trademark owner and/or its licensee. Printed in the U.S.A.

◄ Detach card and mail today! No stamp needed. ◄

Send For
2 FREE BOOKS
Today!

I accept your offer!

Please send me two
free novels and two mystery
gifts (gifts worth about $10).
I understand that these books
are completely free—even
the shipping and handling will
be paid—and I am under no
obligation to purchase anything,
ever, as explained on the back
of this card.

154/354 HDL GJAE

Please Print

FIRST NAME

LAST NAME

ADDRESS

APT.#   CITY

STATE/PROV.   ZIP/POSTAL CODE

Visit us online at
www.ReaderService.com

Offer limited to one per household and not applicable to series that subscriber is currently receiving.
Your Privacy—The Reader Service is committed to protecting your privacy. Our Privacy Policy is available
online at www.ReaderService.com or upon request from the Reader Service. We make a portion of our mailing
list available to reputable third parties that offer products we believe may interest you. If you prefer that we not
exchange your name with third parties, or if you wish to clarify or modify your communication preferences, please
visit us at www.ReaderService.com/consumerschoice or write to us at Reader Service Preference Service, P.O. Box
9062, Buffalo, NY 14240-9062. Include your complete name and address.

AR-815-GF15

© 2015 HARLEQUIN ENTERPRISES LIMITED. ® and ™® are trademarks owned and used by the trademark owner and/or its licensee. Printed in the U.S.A.

◄ Detach card and mail today. No stamp needed. ◄

"OLYMPIA, DINNER," SPENCE SAID through her closed door. She didn't answer, so he knocked and then opened the door. They would be sharing the master bedroom now. He was still wrapping his head and gonads around that one. She lay curled up tight on the bed, her face pale. He rushed to her. "What's wrong? Is it the baby?"

"I think you were right. The double-chocolate ice cream... Oh, God, I think I'm going to be sick." She clutched her middle.

Spence hauled her out of the bed and to the bathroom. She lay on the floor and complained that she was hot, then cold, so he covered her with towels. He glanced over his shoulder and saw a wide-eyed Calvin. "She's okay, buddy. Pregnant ladies have delicate stomachs."

"I didn't want her to get sick."

"Is she okay?" Rickie popped up behind Calvin. "What happened?"

"Don't worry, Calvin. She said that she had too much Dairy Queen ice cream. Why don't you two go check on dinner? Make sure we aren't going to burn the place down." Rickie turned slowly, leading a reluctant Calvin down the hall. Spence refocused on Olympia, who was biting her lip. "*Are* you okay?" Spence whispered, reaching out to brush the sweaty bangs from her forehead.

She nodded. "I thought I was over the morning sickness. Guess I was wrong."

"How about I get you back to bed?"

She didn't answer him, except to squeeze her eyes tightly closed. "Spence, maybe something's wrong. I haven't been sick in a while."

"You're fine. You've gone to the doctor, and she said everything was good."

"I just feel so bad, and—"

"What?" he asked softly, his body tightening with fear.

"I don't know. It's just different, and my—" Her words stopped, and she moaned in misery. "I'm such a baby."

Spence didn't know what to do with this Olympia. This weak and unsure Olympia. He took her hands and squeezed. "You said it. Too much ice cream. What did you expect, eating like a six-year-old?"

She shook her head slowly. "The baby doesn't want me as her mother. I knew I'd be a bad mother."

"It's just what happens to pregnant women. Getting sick—even the whole way through the pregnancy— has nothing to do with the baby thinking you're not a good mother. What about your sisters? You've raised them just fine."

"Anyone would have been better than our mother."

"I'm not going to argue with you." He smiled when her eyes popped open. "Don't faint. I really won't argue with you. I'll help you to bed, then I'll bring you a selt- zer." He put his hand under her elbow and made her sit up. Then he suggested she breathe in and out a few times before encouraging her to her feet and back to their room. He got her settled under the blankets, with the wastebasket, then felt her forehead to be sure she didn't have a fever.

She turned away and said, "It's just the baby."

"Watch it or I'll sausage you."

"What? I'm not up for any—"

"Good Lord, no. I meant tuck the covers in really tight. I do that to Calvin all the time. When he was a baby, it sometimes was the only way to get him to stop crying. Don't tell him I told you. It would embarrass him."

"I won't tell him. I'll just lie here until it's better. Why did I get double fudge?"

He waited until her eyes closed and paused a moment to gather himself and put on a happy face for Calvin and Rickie. Her paleness worried him. If she didn't feel better in the morning, she was going to the doctor's. No argument.

OLYMPIA CURLED INTO a ball of misery. The low, dull ache in her back had moved up to a sharp pain that had started to worry her somewhere deep down. She'd downloaded a couple of pregnancy ebooks, and her symptoms weren't that unusual but... She wouldn't think about that. Her doctor had told her that some women had morning sickness all day and throughout their pregnancy. The medicine had been working so well, she'd nearly forgotten how bad it could be. Maybe the chocolate ice cream, double hot fudge, brownie chunks and chocolate sprinkles hadn't been the best choice. Could you get chocolate poisoning?

Hours—minutes?—later, the nausea eased enough that Olympia could move her head and reposition herself. She hadn't done anything out of the ordinary today. She and Cal had worked with Pasquale, to Cal's delight. The kid just wanted to be normal, not some pasty-faced geek. She'd been careful—helmet, boots and long pants—and Pasquale had been a lamb. Maybe she should offer him to Jessie for her program. When Olympia was on the road with the rodeo, she wouldn't be able to have stock that didn't earn its keep.

Oh, God, it was starting again. The wave of sickness roiled through her. She clamped her mouth closed on the queasiness and the increasing ache in her back. Then, suddenly and blessedly, the nausea got better.

She curled back into her ball, protecting her belly and easing the ache in her back. Could she get Spence to give her a massage? No. That was playing with fire. Even as miserable as she was, the thought of his hands on her made her remember their nights in bed—not many, but enough to store up a list of amazing memories. Her mom had never been sick like this, which might explain why she'd done it four times. Olympia couldn't imagine how she was going to get through this one.

Her guts tightened in fear. Was she losing the baby? Was that why she was so sick? She'd kept saying she didn't want Peanut, but... She'd been at the doctor's just two weeks ago, and they'd both been pronounced healthy. She sucked in a deep breath. She'd seen a program on the morning news that deep breathing cured nearly everything from nausea to depression to cancer... or something. Breathe in, breathe out. She told herself to concentrate on that and not the heaving that had started in her stomach again. If she could just relax, the sharp pains radiating out from her back and down the front of her thighs would go away, too.

"Olympia," Spence said softly from the doorway. "I have the seltzer and a buttered tortilla." He clinked the ice in the glass.

"No," she said, but it came out on a sharp cry as the pain shot through her.

"Where does it hurt?" he asked, hurrying across the small room. "Is it the baby?"

No. It *had* to be something else.

"Talk to me," he said, his face close to hers, his fingers interlaced with hers over her belly. "If you can't tell me what's going on, I'm calling 911."

"No," she protested. "I'm fine. Just all that chocolate."

He stood up and looked down at her, his face set in lines she couldn't read. "Drink your seltzer."

"Not now."

He set the drink on the bedside table and left the room. She closed her eyes, telling herself that being alone was what she wanted. She needed to remember that this was all pretend and temporary. They were not a couple. Cal was not her little boy. She tried to laugh, and it ended on a gasp as another pain rolled through her. Could she make it to the kitchen where she kept her aspirin? What had the doctor told her she could take? Her brain was muzzy from the pain and the nausea, except that little part that insisted something was wrong. She told the scaredy-cat voice to shut up. But, oh, God, she hurt. A sharp pain tightened her stomach. She tried to sit up and another one hit her. She curled tighter. No. Not the baby. She didn't want to lose the baby.

"Something's wrong, Payson," Spence said frantically but quietly into his cell so Calvin and Rickie wouldn't hear. The two of them were sprawled on the broken-down couch in the living room, watching a cartoon that was probably inappropriate. His blood pulsed hard in his ears, making it difficult to hear what his brother was saying.

"Spence," Payson's voice came through, harsh and loud. "Call the ambulance. Don't fool around with this.

It sounds like something more than morning sickness. Get off the phone and call now. Once you do that—"

Spence hung up and dialed 911. He didn't care that his voice wavered as he described the situation and their address. The operator explained that it would take extra time for an ambulance because of a string of accidents on the 10 and a large fire in the historic Presidio district. She suggested calmly that he call the doctor, too.

He hung up and called Olympia's obstetrician, reaching the after-hours operator, barely able to write down the on-call service number. His hands were shaking badly. He tried the number, and the operator who answered said the doctor would get back to him as soon as possible. "How soon is that?" Spence snapped.

"As soon as she can," the operator said soothingly.

He hung up on her, too.

"An ambulance is on the way," he said as he entered Olympia's bedroom. Instead of lying in a fetal ball, she had gotten herself sitting, hunched over and holding her belly. *Oh, God, it's worse.*

"Spence," she groaned, her voice little more than a whisper. "I think it's the baby."

"I know." He shot across the room and pulled her into his arms. "I know. The ambulance may take… I called Payson…your doctor…"

Olympia sucked in a breath and hissed out a moan as every muscle in her body tightened.

They couldn't wait. She was losing the baby now. He had to get her to the hospital. He slid his hands under her knees to pick her up, and she struggled. "Shh. It's all right. We're going to take my truck. We'll be there faster than any ambulance."

"I can walk."

"No. You can't. You can't even straighten up."

"Aah…" she moaned, a long, deep sound that made the hairs on the back of his neck lift. No more talking. He hurried to the truck and laid her in the king cab before going back for Calvin. The little boy for once didn't say anything, but his eyes were round and frightened. Rickie kept quiet, too. He didn't even suggest that she stay at the house.

"She'll be fine. It's just that all the ambulances are tied up. They said to take her instead of waiting," he lied. "I'm sure it's something silly."

Calvin and Rickie both crawled into the back with Olympia. Spence couldn't listen to the soothing comments his son made or he'd end up bawling like a lost calf.

This baby may have started as a mistake, but that didn't mean Spence didn't want her…or him. His hands white-knuckled the steering wheel as he raced to the hospital. Why hadn't the doctor called back? She should meet them at the hospital. *Damn.* He'd forgotten the phone. His fear moved close to panic.

"Daddy," Calvin said, his voice quavering. "Limpy's crying."

"Hurry up. Can't this stupid truck go faster?" Rickie said in a shaky voice.

"It's okay. She'll be okay." Now Spence could hear Olympia's whimpers, and he pushed harder on the accelerator, cursing when they got stopped at another traffic signal.

"Stop swearing," Olympia croaked. "You're freaking out Cal. Even Rickie doesn't know some of those."

"Sorry, buddy," he said, looking in the rearview mirror at the big eyes of his son. "It'll be all right. Just a few more minutes, then the doctors will take care of everything."

"I don't want the baby to die," Calvin said.

"That won't happen. I won't let it happen. That's what daddies do. They make sure nothing bad happens, so you don't need to worry."

"That's not the way it works," Rickie said quietly.

Spence glanced one more time in the mirror, wanting to reassure Rickie. To reassure himself. He made a sharp right to get off the main drag, hoping that the backstreets and alleys would get him to the hospital faster. He couldn't lose their baby. He couldn't lose Olympia. Somewhere over the past two months, they'd gotten lodged in his heart as firmly as Calvin was. The thought of anything happening to them made adrenaline-laced fear fill every one of his cells. *Get them to the hospital. Now.*

Chapter Ten

The tight grip of Calvin's hand on hers and the quiet but constant swearing from Spence took Olympia's mind off her own pain and fear. She might not want to be a mom, but that didn't mean she wanted anything to happen to little Peanut. She clutched at her middle, hoping to hold everything just where it was. She felt a ripple of muscle. Contractions? No. Not labor. She had months and months to go.

"Ten minutes," Spence said over his shoulder as he raced through residential neighborhoods, ignoring stop signs and one ways. God, she hoped they survived the trip.

Cal squeezed her hand again as another wussy whimper escaped her. She smiled at him. "I'm okay. Just what happens when you have chocolate poisoning."

"Poison," he gasped.

"Shut up, Limpy," her sister snapped, her eyes slits of fear and anger. "Don't joke."

"Sorry," Olympia said in a hoarse whisper. "But I bet if Cal did a search he could find out how much chocolate is deadly." She turned her head so her sister and Cal wouldn't see the tears that leaked out of her eyes.

Rickie pounded on the back of Spence's seat and yelled, "Hurry. She's delirious."

Olympia closed her eyes as the pain no longer had a start or stop. Her back, her thighs, everything from her breastbone south hurt with a cramping ache ten times worse than a charley horse.

"Mrs. MacCormack." Olympia cracked her eyes open as a woman shouted into her face.

"Olympia," she corrected.

"Olympia. You're at Tucson General. We just need to get you set up on an IV. But you need to keep your eyes open."

"Why?" Olympia asked, closing her eyes against the pain.

"Olympia. Open up," the woman insisted.

Olympia forced her lids upward and the room swam. She swallowed. "The baby."

"You're both okay. Once the doctor sees the scan, we'll know more. Right now, we're giving you something that should stop the contractions. You're lucky you didn't wait any longer to come in, or we might not have—"

"I don't care," Spence's voice rang out. "She's my wife." All-American, boy-next-door Spence looked like something between an avenging angel and a serial killer as he bulled his way into her room. She held her shaking hand out to him and he grabbed hold, the warmth of his palm anchoring her.

"Mr. MacCormack, I need to—"

"You can do it while I'm here." Spence's gaze locked on hers, the dusty-blue desert eyes steady but dark with as much pain as her own heart felt.

"The baby..."

"The baby is fine." His other hand snaked out and

onto her abdomen. "The doctors said they can stop the labor."

"Labor?"

"The backaches, the nausea…it was early labor."

"Oh," she said, looking at the bag of liquid dripping into her arm.

"Medication to stop the contractions, then we'll see where we stand." His hand tightened on hers, and now she saw the brightness of tears in his eyes.

"Spence, I'm scared." That hadn't been what she'd meant to say.

He pulled her into his arms. "Me, too, but I'm not going to let our baby die. No matter what, I won't let anything happen to you or our baby."

She wanted to hug him back, but her arms were so heavy and the IV wouldn't let her move. "Promise." She heard the nurses saying something, but she wasn't letting him go.

"Promise. Cross my heart. Stick a needle in my eye."

She tried to smile. Then Spence leaned over to kiss her forehead. As she drifted off, the nurse scolded him, while Spence went all lawyer on her ass…hiney.

"Mr. MacCormack, your son…"

Spence turned toward the voice and saw Calvin and Rickie standing by a woman in scrubs. The little guy's cheeks glistened with tears, and Rickie's face shone white in the harsh lighting. Spence opened his arms to both of them. Calvin slammed into him, sobs shaking his thin, fragile body. Rickie buried her face into his shoulder. Spence's own eyes burned with tears, too. He feared giving into his own barely checked sobs because if he started, there'd be no way he could stop. *Dad up.*

"It's okay, buddy," he said, patting his son's narrow back. "Rickie, she's going to be fine."

"Limpy and the baby—" Calvin started.

"They're getting medicine right now. The doctors are going to make them better." God, he hoped so.

"Are you sure, Daddy?"

"How the hell can you be sure?" Rickie barked.

"No swearing." He steadied himself. "Olympia is napping right now. We'll see her in just a little bit." Calvin snuggled into Spence, grasping him tighter, but the sobs had stopped. Spence maneuvered them out of the room, and Rickie stepped away, wiping at her face. He crouched down and rocked Calvin as he'd done when he was a baby, when his breathing had sometimes gotten stuck because of his heart. When he heard the little boy squeak, Spence loosened his tight hold.

"Mr. MacCormack," a female voice said from his right. "We need to get the insurance information now that your wife is settled."

Spence stood slowly and picked Calvin up, the little boy's legs and arms wrapping around him. Calvin hadn't let him hold him like this since he'd had his surgery. Once again, they both needed that comfort. He wanted to do the same for Rickie, but she stood stiffly beside him. He'd get the paperwork done, then he'd call Lavonda to come get the kids. He'd beg Jessie's sister to stay at the ranch to keep Rickie in line, look after Calvin and take care of the stock while he and Olympia were at the hospital.

AFTER GETTING ONLY snatches of sleep on the foldout torture chair beside Olympia's bed, Spence's eyelids rasped like sandpaper. His stand-up-to-anything cowgirl looked small in the bed, a doctor staring sternly down at her. Color had made its way back into her face, but she lay too quietly. Her meek compliance worried Spence. He didn't totally believe she'd be fine.

"We're out of the woods for right now. The baby is safe," the doctor said.

Olympia clutched at Spence's hand.

"But," Dr. Neiman said, her small dark eyes narrowed, "you were lucky. I'm putting you on complete bed rest. We'll keep you in the hospital another day to make sure the contractions have stopped and your cervix hasn't opened, then you can go home."

"Bed rest," Olympia said.

"Yes. That means the only time your feet are on the floor is when you have to use the bathroom. Not to check on your horses, not to make a meal, nothing else. You need to keep the baby in there."

"But—"

"No buts," Spence said. Why was she arguing? "You'll do what she says. I know that you didn't want this baby—"

"I would never do anything to hurt the baby." Her hand stroked her belly. "It's just that I know I'm not mom material. Peanut would be better off without me."

Dr. Neiman cut in. "No arguing. This is a very serious situation, Olympia. You," the doctor said pointing at Spence, "need to get home and get some sleep. You're exhausted. You need to see your son, calm down her sister, who's called here no less than twenty times, and get the house ready for Olympia to come home. Can her sister help with your son and the horses?"

"A friend is coming in." He closed his eyes for a moment and swayed, catching himself on the bed.

The doctor laid a long cool hand on his forearm and said softly, "She's fine. The baby's fine. Remember that when she goes a little crazy cooped up in the bed."

"Okay." He didn't know what else to say and feared that if he said much more he'd start crying—not the best way to convince the doctor or Olympia that he was a competent male head of household.

"You can go. Rickie can come and get me. I know you can't afford to miss any work," Olympia said as soon as the doctor walked out.

"I've got time." Bald-faced lie, but she didn't need to know that. This was important. This was his baby... their baby. "I need to check on Calvin and Rickie and make sure that Lavonda is okay or if I need to call in reinforcements. It's all temporary. I can't expect Lavonda to watch Calvin and take care of the ranch. I know I wanted him full-time, but this isn't exactly how I pictured it."

"This is definitely not what I signed up for, either. I can't look for a barrel racer and start training." She sucked in a shaky breath. "And I'm going to look like the Pillsbury Doughboy if I'm stuck in bed."

He stared at her, seeing the real distress on her face. How could she think of any of that when their child was at risk? "It'll be worth it when we have the baby."

"Hah." She barked out a short laugh.

"You won't be pregnant forever," he tried.

"It feels that way."

A laugh escaped him, because for a few seconds, she'd sounded just like Calvin when he was frustrated by a LEGO design that didn't turn out the way he'd planned.

"Don't laugh," she snapped.

"I'm sorry, and I'm sorry you'll be stuck in bed. It won't be for that long."

"Long enough."

"What do you want me to do?"

"Turn back the clock and find a condom that doesn't break."

"Can't do that, because then I wouldn't have my new son or daughter."

"Daughter," she said quietly.

"Excuse me?"

"They told me that the baby is a little girl."

A girl. His chest tightened as he thought about a little girl with solemn dark eyes and her mother's quick smile. A little girl fearlessly riding a pony and punching her brother in the arm. "I think Calvin would like a little sister."

He sat down in the torture chair and took Olympia's hand. "I know this isn't how we mapped out our time together, but we'll make it through. Both you and the baby are safe, and that's all that matters to me." He squeezed her hand to reassure himself as much as her.

"I know I sound selfish and mean and petty...but... I've waited years and years to do...well, to run away to the rodeo. Every time I had to pay for my sisters' clothes or doctor visits, I'd remind myself that one day they'd be grown and then I could do what I wanted, and all I ever wanted was to go on the road as a barrel racer. I traded cleaning stables for riding lessons. I competed a little bit when my sisters didn't need the money. I wouldn't be so close now if I hadn't gotten the money for Rickie from you. But the baby... A baby was *never* in my plans. After competing, winning a couple of championships, I was going to open my own riding and training school at the ranch, then ride the senior circuit. I had it all figured out."

He heard the tears in her voice, the sadness and the desperation. "Once you have the baby and recover, you can do all that. I told you I'll take care of our... daughter, and she won't know who her mother is. Are you still sure about that?" His lawyer brain kicked his other brain because he had the paperwork that made the new baby his, no matter what. Why was he trying to change her mind?

She remained silent, shaking her head. "I can't. It's not that I hate either you or Cal. It's just—"

"I know. The rodeo. Jessie was planning on doing rodeo and having kids."

"Maybe. And I know there are other women who do it, but not when they were starting out."

He stayed quiet, letting his mind settle as he tried to figure out what to say. "I know we have the contract, but that doesn't mean I don't want you to be happy."

"You think being a mom will make me happy?"

He shrugged. "I don't want you to regret any of this down the road."

"How could I regret it when it's what I've always wanted?"

"I always wanted to be a district attorney, until we had Calvin. Then I realized how many hours out of the day I'd be away, and I changed my mind." He stared at her face, taking in the paleness and tightness around her beautiful tabby-cat eyes. "I'm still a lawyer, and I love what I do, and the hours are more reasonable." She gave him a look. "Usually."

"But if I'm not a barrel racer...a cowgirl...then what

am I? Just some woman with kids, married to a successful lawyer."

"You're Olympia James MacCormack."

"That's just a name. Not who I am. What I am." Tears shone in her eyes, then spilled down her cheeks. He sat on the bed and pulled her to him, ignoring the tubes and her little squeak of protest. He stroked her hair until he felt her relax against him. He didn't know what to say. The silver-tongued lawyer had absolutely zero words. He patted her shoulder one last time and sat back enough to see that the tears had dried. "I'll be back later, and we'll talk more."

Coward, his little voice mocked him. *Heck, yes*, he told that darned voice. He needed a nap, and more than that he had to hug Calvin to remind himself what he was fighting for. But was that all he was fighting for now?

Chapter Eleven

Olympia opened the cabinet looking for vanilla pudding to dip the spicy tortilla chips in. Yum. Since getting off bed rest and feeling better than she had in months, she'd not been able to stop eating this pregnancy-induced combo. That wouldn't have been so bad, except Spence just had to point that the chips had three times the daily recommended amount of sodium whenever she complained that her shoes were tight. He just had to be right *and* couldn't keep it to himself.

The slider squealed open. She started guiltily. Thank goodness it was Lavonda, who wouldn't say a word or even give her the "look." The other woman had become a good friend during Olympia's bed rest. "I'm glad it's you."

"Why's that? Besides the fact that you're eating all Cal's pudding."

"I'm going stir crazy. I know Spence told you that I'm confined to quarters because I was a little dizzy last night. I did the weeks of bed rest like the doctor ordered. I'm fine. I don't know why he gets so unreasonable."

"Really, you're complaining because someone is waiting on you hand and foot?" said the petite dark-haired woman, who looked like the corporate power-house she used to be, even in boots and jeans.

"Waiting on me hand and foot includes making me eat kale and sardines. Yuck."

"Spence has been looking things up online again."

"He says they're good for the baby." Olympia looked down. Six weeks after the scare, and her belly had gone from respectable bump to basketball status. Within forty-eight hours of getting home, Spence had gone out and bought her maternity clothing. Lucky for her he'd taken Rickie and Lavonda.

Her friend pulled the plastic cup from Olympia's hand and pushed her toward the living room. "Go sit down. I'm getting myself a soda and you water. Rickie and Cal are pulling weeds and rearranging the tack room. I have my orders from the boss man, and it's to make sure you sit around with your feet up—and they must be sore if you're wearing Rickie's awful almost Uggs."

Olympia refused to look down.

"Jeez," Lavonda said, "don't cry. I didn't mean to make you cry."

Olympia waved her hand. Today was a bad weepy day. She'd had to turn off the TV when the animal-rescue ads had come on. "Other than my sister and Cal, how is everything? Muffin sorted out? We need to get that horse adopted."

"I don't know," Lavonda said. "He's messed up. It's not as if I've never been around a horse that bites first and asks questions later, but…"

"A little more time. He's just so sure that we're going to treat him badly." Olympia landed on the couch and put her feet up on the ottoman. Lavonda handed her water and plopped down in the recliner with an iced tea.

"Jessie and I've been talking," Lavonda continued. "We've decided that it's time for an intervention."

"Intervention? Is this about the pudding?"

"Not this time, but I think Cal will ask me to do that one before long. He's tired of being out of pudding." Lavonda took a long sip of tea. Olympia's worry moved up two notches, and Peanut did a double roll and poke. "Why are you and Spence still pretending that this is a fake marriage?"

"Not fake. Elvis married us for real. It's just that we have the prenup and addendum for getting out of the marriage gracefully." She wanted to pat herself on the back for how steadily she'd said that. She'd nearly told Spence to tear up the darned agreement when she'd been in the hospital, which would have been stupid, stupid, stupid, especially since they'd never talked later as he'd promised they would.

Lavonda sat up straight and set down her glass. "You're sharing a bedroom."

"But not like that." Not because she said no. He didn't offer.

"You've obviously done that at some point."

"Obviously, but that one night does not mean we're a couple or anything."

"Possibly. But you're also raising two kids and have another on the way."

"Rickie is my sister, and she's leaving in a few weeks." That choked Olympia up, and she almost didn't hear what Lavonda said next.

"If you two don't figure out your relationship soon,

we're going to lock you in a secluded cabin and not let you out until you go into labor."

"Excuse me. Are you trying a *Parent Trap*?"

"We're desperate."

"Spence and I are okay with the way we've set things up. We'll explain everything to Cal and Rickie. Soon."

"I've seen the way you two look at each other. It was there before you ended up in the hospital, but after that, it's gotten stronger. You two have changed."

"By changed, you mean that Spence now feels he has the right to be a dictator?"

"We're friends, so I'm just going to say this. Apparently, lack of sex makes you mean and nasty and a pudding-eating machine." Olympia felt a flush of embarrassment race up her face. Her danged body had always acted out of her control around him. After breaking down in the hospital, she'd thought they would finally talk out whatever had been happening between them. Instead, Spence worked longer hours, made more rules about what she could do, slept on the floor and left the house most days before any of them were awake.

Lavonda stared hard at Olympia, her dark eyes intense. "I watched the same thing with Payson and Jessie. I know what lack of bedroom gymnastics does, what denying love—"

"Love?"

"Yes. My God, you two are so obvious. There's a whole lot more between you than a baby, a little boy, a sister and a ranch."

"Yeah. A hundred-page agreement."

"That was then. This is now…and to be honest, you two would never have signed that if you hadn't felt something for each other. Neither of you are the kind of people who do one-night stands."

"Are you trying to make me feel worse?"

"I'm trying to help you see what all of us see, which has nothing to do with that agreement. What about Cal and your sister and especially the new baby?"

"Cal wasn't supposed to be here, and neither was Rickie."

"Life's like that, isn't it? It happens when you have other plans. Are those other plans really working for you now? I know you haven't talked to that cowgirl up in Flagstaff who's got a string of barrel racers she's looking to unload. What have you got? A little more than three months until you have the baby?"

"A lot has been going on."

Lavonda's snort sounded a lot like Muffin's. "I know that you're not the kind of woman to say one thing and do another…generally. I'm just reminding you of that now. Maybe you and Spence need to throw away those hundred pages of nonsense."

"That's the only reason we've stayed together."

"Really? Why do you think he married you?"

"Because he knew me and I was single."

"He knows a lot of women, including single ones."

"He knew I was desperate for money. He—"

"The two of you had unfinished business and you know it. You still do. You're both so worried about what you *think* you should do that you're missing out on what you have to do to be happy. And not just you, everyone else's happiness is tied up in this, too."

"This is just what I was trying to avoid. I've put off everything that I've wanted to do for other people."

"You've sacrificed for your sisters. No doubt about it. But why? You could have left. You could've moved on."

"Who would have taken care of them?"

"Your mom, foster parents, one of your other sisters." Lavonda stood and finished her iced tea. "You know all this. You're a cowgirl who does the tough stuff, and none of this is tough stuff. This is what you want."

"No. It's not."

"Really? You can look at Spence and not think about what you two did at the wedding? You can look at Cal and not think about being there when he gets his first girlfriend, starts to drive—"

"But I've waited… I've promised—"

"You were promising yourself to be happy and to have what *you* wanted. Now, what do you really want? To live on the road and race? I've done it. It's not as glamorous as you'd think. Or do you want to sleep every night with Spence and work with him to raise your children on this ranch?"

Olympia hauled herself off the couch. While her discussion with Spence at the hospital had made her think about staying with him and the kids, she couldn't give up on the dream that had gotten her through those cold dark nights in the trailer. Could she still rodeo with the kids? She wasn't convinced.

"I've got to go. Big doings at Hope's Ride that only a PR guru like myself can take care of."

Olympia watched her friend leave. What did any of this mean? That Lavonda and Jessie were nosy. That the two of them thought they knew best but didn't.

"Limpy," Cal yelled from the kitchen. "Where are my pudding cups? You promised."

She burst into tears. "I ate all of them," she sobbed.

Cal appeared in front of her, taking her hand. "It's okay. I'll have fruit." His face twisted in disgust.

Now laughter rolled through her. God, the roller coaster of emotions wouldn't stop. She knew that she was going crazy. She had to be. It was just that Cal's dear little face looked so noble in his fruit-eating sacrifice. Could it be that she really wanted to be here for him and the new baby?

"I'm calling Dad," her stepson said.

"No," Olympia said, putting her hand on her stomach and calming herself. "This is normal. Let's go to the store and get more pudding. It'll be our secret."

"I know Dad thinks pudding is bad for the baby, but I checked. It's got calcium, so that's good."

"You're a good big brother," she said, and choked up a little. But she didn't feel trapped. She could see a new child and Cal playing together, and that didn't make her want to run, but she wasn't sure that it made her want to stay, either.

IN THE BEDROOM, waiting for Spence to get home, her back ached and her feet itched. Tears leaked from her eyes. He'd called hours ago to say that he'd be home late. Olympia knew he was logging extra hours to make up for missed work and to bank goodwill for when the baby was born. Peanut was actually snoozing. Usually, when Olympia lay down, the baby woke up, but the pudding cups had done the trick. Olympia and Cal had laid in a good supply, hiding the cache at the back of the hall closet.

"Why aren't you asleep?" Spence whispered as he opened the door and she started, twisting her body. The movement shot a zing of electric pain up her back, forcing out a high-pitched squeak. "Do I need to call the doctor?" he demanded as he sat down on the side of the bed, his hand going to the baby bump.

"It's nothing." She didn't move his hand as she pushed against the bed to sit up. "You startled me. Just pulled on a muscle. Too much lying around like a lump of lard."

He still didn't move away. "How long were you in the barn?"

"I wasn't—"

"Don't lie. I can smell it."

"I walked out with Cal after dinner. He wanted to show me the braid he'd done in Pasquale's mane. If you'd been here, he'd have taken you instead."

He stretched out beside her, leaning against the headboard. She noticed that his hair needed a trim and the line between his brows had deepened. "Sorry," he breathed out. "I know I haven't been around much—"

She pinched her arm hard to distract herself and to stop the tears from falling, a trick she'd learned as a child. His gaze, darkened with emotion, stayed on her face. She swallowed hard. "Lavonda thinks that I don't want to rodeo." Peanut did a somersault and her stomach full of pudding gurgled unpleasantly.

"What does she think you want?" Spence asked slowly, averting his gaze.

"Never mind. I don't know why I told you that. What difference does it make what she thinks?"

"Why don't you tell me? You brought it up."

"Stop being such a lawyer," she accused. He had a nice life all mapped out, and it didn't include a trailer-trash cowgirl who thought ramen noodles were foreign food.

"Since I am a lawyer, that's a specious argument."

She knew better than most women that happily ever after and men sticking around to be a daddy just didn't happen, except in fairy-tale movies. The tears streamed down her face faster.

"Shh. We'll work this out."

"I've dreamed about the rodeo, about leaving Arizona since I was a little girl," she insisted...to him... to herself.

"I know, but maybe now is the time to give up on that exact dream and face the reality of—"

"I've faced down plenty of reality. I was the one who called the ambulance when my sister got so sick she hallucinated," she said through her tears into the softness of his shirt. "I was the one the police called when they picked Mama up DUI."

"Oh, honey," he said softly into her hair as she curled into his side, her face fitting perfectly against his shoulder. Those broad, strong shoulders could stand straight against anything. "I'm sorry you had to do that. You're amazing, to have lived through all that and not only come out a brave cowgirl but to have raised your sisters to be good women, too."

"I'm crying my eyes out here. Not very brave," she said, pressing harder into his shoulder as the tears slowed.

"Brave," he insisted. "You married a stranger for your sister. You took on this ranch. You took on my son, and you took on Muffin and his love of pastries." She gave a soggy laugh, and he squeezed her tighter. "Tell me why you don't want to rodeo."

She sucked in a breath, trying to organize her thoughts. "It's not an easy life, you know." Could it really be that her dream had been wrong all these years? That she'd been focusing on something she'd never actually wanted? "When I was little, I read this book about a famous cowgirl. How she was an orphan and was adopted by a family who made her sleep in the barn and work the horses and cows all the time. She went on to win bronc riding and owned her own ranch. She said that she never let anything or anyone turn her from her goals and her dreams. I wanted to be just like her."

"She earned the money for everything from the rodeo, so you—"

"Yes, but that's not why I wanted to rodeo. She talked about how when she was bronc riding or barrel racing or roping, there wasn't anything but what was in front of her. Her past was gone. When she was in the ring, she wasn't the little orphan girl. I didn't want to be one of those James girls. I wanted to leave that in the past."

"You have. You're a MacCormack now."

"Don't," she said, trying to pull away. Spence held on tight.

"I'm sorry. I shouldn't have joked about that. I can only imagine your childhood, and I can see why the rodeo would appeal. You can still do that with the kids. We could work it out. Maybe a new agreement?" His dimple showed.

"Maybe that was a little girl's dream and now I'm a woman?" She'd been going over their talk at the hospital again and again.

"That you are," he said, giving her butt a squeeze.

She didn't know whether to laugh or moan, whether to be offended or excited. "Aren't you supposed to be sleeping on the floor?"

"I will." He didn't move his hand. "It's for the best, after our scare."

That cowgirl had said the rodeo made her forget everything. That happened when Olympia and Spence made love. His kisses and soft touches caused everything to fade away. She snuggled into him. Was it wrong to want that again? His arm came around her more firmly, pulling her tightly against him.

"I shouldn't," he whispered, then said to her, "What do you need, cowgirl?"

"You."

He turned slowly to her, giving her plenty of time to pull away. She arched a little, pressing her aching breasts against him. She wanted him. She needed him.

Burying his face in the space between her breasts, he whispered, "I don't want to know where you start and I end. I've kept myself away from you as long as I can."

She could tell he was being careful with her, so she moaned in his ear that he needed to touch her as if he meant it. Olympia grabbed Spence's thick hair, holding him to her. She didn't want his clever mouth to stop its sensual search, except that space between her legs ached for him, too. She wanted him to take her hard and fast, then come back to her for slow loving when this first flush of heat had been quenched. She grabbed his one hand and placed it on the ache, urging him with an arching back to touch her, pleasure her.

He lifted her with no effort, arching his own hips into her as she came down on top of him. This was better than any bronc riding could be, than the dust and the screams of the rodeo. It took a moment for them to find the rhythm, but when they did, the pleasure built until there was nothing but white-hot heat and Spence.

HE STROKED HER sweat-darkened hair from her temple, kissing her there as she shifted into a better position against him, obviously languid and content, from the purr she gave him. "You're some cowgirl," he whispered huskily.

"You're not a bad cowboy," she said around a yawn. "Maybe next time you'll last more than eight seconds."

He chuckled. "That's the cow calling the bull black."

She tilted back her head and opened one eye. "That makes absolutely no sense."

"Hush and go to sleep." He smiled into her hair, not wanting anything to intrude on these moments of happiness. Too soon the reality of their lives would be back, along with worries about what they had just done, what it meant…or didn't mean.

"You know," she whispered. "That cowgirl—the famous one—must never have met the right cowboy if she thought the rodeo was the only way to find pleasure."

Chapter Twelve

Olympia walked to the mailbox because it was about the only chore Spence still let her do. Looking down, she could see the drive in front of her but not her feet. She hadn't been able to see them for more than a month. Less than eight weeks and she'd have the baby. The doctor could be precise because Olympia knew exactly when Peanut had been conceived. Lily Grace? Did she feel like a Lily Grace? Nope. Olympia tried to suck in a deep breath. Nope. Not happening.

The sight of the mailbox gave her a thrill. Jeez, her life was pathetic. She walked…waddled now. It was nearly over, and then what? She and Spence had been sharing not only a room but also the delightfully springy bed for more than three months now. Really, it had only been fair to Spence. Sleeping on the floor was ridiculous. They'd also both agreed again that the sex did not make their contract null and void. In fact, they'd also agreed that having the legal document made it easier to enjoy each other without getting their messy emotions involved. So sometimes they did more than sleep. Other times, he held her and they talked about their days, the baby, the pain of stepping on a LEGO piece. By some unspoken agreement, they did not talk about the future, which was fine. Really.

She pulled the junk mail out and considered just leaving it there. Carrying those few extra ounces back to the house felt like too much, even though the doctor had told her that she'd probably gain another six to seven pounds. At this rate, she'd be as broad as she was tall. Spence would need to widen every chair in the house to fit her. She tried to stretch the kink out of her back. *Stop whining*, she told herself firmly.

She gathered all the mail and started slowly up the drive. Think of the nap she'd take in a little bit. That was about all she did—sleep, eat and get fatter. She shook her head. With Cal in school and Rickie at college, Olympia couldn't believe how empty the house felt. It also gave her time to think, inevitably about the baby. Not that she was surprised. With the limits on her activity, the constant bathroom trips, heartburn, swollen ankles... What else could she think about?

There were times she thought she'd come to terms with staying on the ranch and raising the baby on her own. Other times she imagined the ranch with Spence and both kids. Her make-believe future rarely included riding rodeo now. The big, huge, elephant-in-the-room problem was what else she'd do. Was raising kids, the thing she'd always promised herself she wouldn't do, enough? Some days, she believed that she and Spence could make a go of the marriage. Obviously, that was the pregnancy brain all the blogs talked about.

She paused to catch her breath. How was she ever going to get back into shape? The women who claimed they jogged and did yoga while pregnant must be cyborgs. Olympia again reminded herself to stop whining and determinedly walked back to the house with the plan that she'd do more than sit around like a big, fat, cranky blob.

"WHERE'S THE MAIL?" Spence asked as she stirred lazily at the pot of stew.

"Over there." She pointed to the place by the phone where she put the mail every day. For a genius lawyer, Spence could be thick. She tried to get upset, but just watching him look through the mail made her want to jump his bones. Pregnancy hormones struck again.

"Crap," he said with feeling.

A bill they'd forgotten to pay? Over the past two months, with the animals to feed and then a cutback in hours at the firm, money had gotten size-ten-foot-in-size-six-boot tight.

"Darn it. I can't believe this. Her parents put her up to this."

Spence had to be talking about his ex. "Is there a problem?"

"Missy—who just got out of rehab—is suing for full permanent custody, plus child support and alimony."

"She hasn't talked to Cal for at least a month."

"I know. Damn," Spence said with feeling. "Calvin has finally settled in and likes his new school." Like Cal, his ears got beet red when he was upset.

"Any judge will see that Cal is better off here. Plus Missy more or less abandoned him. We have a nice home."

"Nothing like her parents' place. Those people have a huge house and a housekeeper, and they can afford a nanny and a tutor."

"That doesn't count because you're his dad. He loves you."

"On paper Missy looks great because she has her family's support."

"You have me and Payson and Jessie and—"

"I have you until you decide to leave."

She opened her mouth to tell him they could change that. Most days she couldn't imagine her life without Spence, Cal and the baby. Then she'd imagine the way it probably would be. Spence leaving her, walking away like men had done to every other James woman. She lamely said, "Which was written so you could get custody of Cal. That's the whole point." She placed her hand on the dancing baby. She couldn't fool Peanut, who did somersaults when her mother got emotional.

He gave her a look she couldn't quite interpret before saying, "I'd better go look up what the truck's worth because I'm going to need the cash to pay the attorney."

"Is it really that bad?"

"Really. I'm paying for your sister's education, for the damned horses' feed, including Pasquale who does nothing but sleep and what about all your doctor's visits and the cost of the hospital?"

"It won't be long until I'm back in the saddle and earning my keep."

He waved her away. "At the rodeo. Right."

"I bet Payson and Jessie could help us with a loan."

"Yeah, just what I want to do, go begging to my big brother."

She didn't answer, stung.

In the quiet, he said, "Soon it won't be your problem anyway. The kids and I will be on our own. I've got to have full, ironclad custody by then or Missy's parents will jump all over me again. I'll be back." Spence slammed the door.

Her spirits sank a little as she thought about the empty house, but then she got mad, realizing that he blamed her for his own plan not working out. She hurried as quickly as she could after him, catching him by his truck. "It won't be my fault if your in-laws...your ex in-laws cause a problem. I've done everything that we agreed to."

"I don't remember being the sole breadwinner as part of any discussions."

Did he work at finding the easiest way to piss her off? She was not a freeloader. She did not sponge off a man. That was her mother. "I have boarders, and I would've helped more, but you said no. I would have gotten a job, too, but I'm stuck here, gestating."

"Gestating? Is that what you call it now? You're pregnant."

"And whose fault is that?" She wanted to punch him—hard.

"You were there, too. At least I'm willing to step up and take responsibility—"

"Of course. Super Spence. Willing to take on everyone's problems and save them from themselves. I don't need you. I could have done this on my own."

"Yeah. How?"

"The same way I've done everything else in my life. I'm not a poor, pathetic woman who can only get along because I hooked up with some man."

"You've made that abundantly clear."

Peanut did a double somersault, and Olympia took in a deep breath. She also took a moment to think about what she'd just been saying. Spence had been out of line, maybe, but she didn't need to attack. They were doing as well as they could, weren't they?

"I really do need to do something about the truck," he said, his back to her. "The payments are huge."

JUST AS SPENCE finished speaking, Calvin yelled from the patio, "Hey, what's for supper? It doesn't smell so good."

Spence didn't move because he didn't want to see Olympia's face. He knew he'd made low blows, but he could lose Calvin. He heard her swear under her breath. He hazarded a glance toward her as she started for the house, wondering why her waddling gait made him feel something between proud and aroused. He was seriously twisted. He caught up to her as she got to the kitchen.

"What the heck are you looking at?" Olympia asked, her tabby-cat eyes narrowed.

"Nothing," he mumbled. His greatest fears were coming true, and all he could think about were his wife's "assets."

"Whatever it was, you made Limpy mad," Calvin said, his expression beginning to look a lot like Olympia's. How was that even possible?

Spence looked over at the stove and said, "Let's forget about whatever was in that pan. I'll spring for Saguaro Sal's."

Calvin hooted his approval. "I get to play six games, right?"

Spence nodded and made sure to not catch Olympia's glare. He'd just been complaining about money, and here he was, throwing it away on dinner and kid-appropriate entertainment.

"Go get dressed in something clean," he said to Calvin. Olympia turned away and put the pan in the sink with a slam.

She frowned. "Saguaro Sal's? You know it's a school night, right? And that it'll cost us about a million dollars."

He shrugged. "We can't eat what you made."

She stiffened. "If you hadn't been attacking me, I would have paid attention to the food. There's plenty in the freezer."

"I can afford to take my family out to an overpriced kiddie paradise." He stomped off, knowing he sounded about as old as Calvin.

"Are you ready?" he asked through his son's open door. "We've got to get going if you want to play Street Fighter and Hedgehog."

"Dad." Calvin sounded pained. "Those are ooold games. Nobody plays those."

"I do. Guess I'm old," he said in a hearty voice, stepping into the boy's room.

"What's wrong, Dad?" Calvin stood in the middle of his room, half in, half out of a T-shirt with a bright neon design that Rickie had bought him at a street fair.

"Nothing."

"You shouldn't lie."

Spence stopped himself from denying it. Calvin was a smart kid, smart enough to know that something was up. "I got a letter and—"

"You fought with Limpy. You shouldn't do that. She's pregnant and…she's nice."

"She is nice," he agreed. "Adults can be nice and not agree."

"Like you and Mommy?"

"Not exactly like me and Mommy. We'll work it out. You don't need to worry, buddy. Adult stuff." Spence tried to ruffle his son's hair, but the boy stepped away.

Calvin looked at him, very serious and very adult. "I know Mimi and Grandpa Stu want me to stay with them. They've said so, but I like it here, even if the hot water doesn't always work. Don't fight with Limpy anymore, Dad, or she might want us to leave."

His son knew exactly how to cut out his guts. Spence choked out, "I won't fight."

"Go apologize, then. That's what you have to do."

His son—his bighearted, big-brained son—was right. He needed to apologize. He'd been wrong to attack Olympia where she was most vulnerable. She'd tried hard to be what he needed. "You're extrasmart tonight."

"Stop being mushy. Go apologize so we can get to Sal's."

He found Olympia still in the kitchen, scrubbing the pan in the sink.

"I want to—"

"Yell at me some more," she sniffed.

Darn it. She was crying. He hadn't meant to make her cry. "I'm sorry," he said as he pulled her away from the sink. "The letter got me all messed up. I'm worried."

"I know that." She sucked in a breath. "I just don't want to make it worse."

"You're not. My God, I couldn't do it without you. You're so good with Calvin."

"It's not me. He doesn't really need me. He's such a—"

"Don't sell yourself short. Calvin still needs a mother…a strong, caring woman in his life."

Olympia patted her belly. Those unconscious movements had increased as the baby grew more active. She'd also softened in some essential way. He could see her bond with the baby and Calvin growing. He was happy but also fearful. Would she really walk away? And if she did, how would he...the kids take it? He couldn't think about that now. Eugenia and Stuart Smythe-Ferris were top of his list.

"Maybe it should be just the guys at Sal's?" she asked as the silence stretched out.

"Are you trying to get out of this? I don't think so. It's not fair to send an adult in there on his own."

"Any other adult, maybe, but I think you like the games more than he does."

With that little exchange, they were back on familiar footing. The affection, the connection, but nothing too deep, because too deep meant that he'd need to face what exactly was going to happen in two months when she had the baby.

"Come on, you two, let's go," Calvin said. "Dad, did you apologize? Limpy, I told him to apologize."

"He did a good job," she told his son. "Are you sure you want me to come along?"

"Of course," Calvin said. "You keep Dad from pouting when I beat him."

"I do not pout. Grown men do not pout."

They argued, teased and laughed the whole way to Sal's. Spence's lawyer brain could pay attention to the games as he turned over not only the letter from his former in-laws but also what was going on between him and his wife. Eugenia and Stuart were easier to deal with.

"Dad," Calvin said with disgust. "Pay attention. I beat you again."

"You're going to be sorry now," Spence joked, focusing on the here and now, because wasn't that why he was doing all this? So he could be with his son?

"Ha! You've got old-man reflexes."

"It's on now, boy."

Calvin beat Spence again. The boy really was good at the video games, which might be more because he'd spent too many hours inside than any brainpower.

"Why doesn't Limpy have a ring?"

"Excuse me?"

"Husbands and wives are supposed to have rings when they're married. You two don't have them."

Kids were great at lobbing these left-field questions. Good thing he had a great attorney face. "We decided we didn't need them."

"Grandpa Stu says that diamonds are a girl's best friend."

"He was being funny. Not all married couples have rings."

Calvin let the comment drop, but Spence couldn't stop thinking about it. Why hadn't they gotten rings? His in-laws would notice it. He should have thought of that.

"What are you frowning about?" Olympia asked as she came up to them.

"How Calvin keeps beating me. I think he must be cheating." Spence definitely didn't want to say anything to her about the rings. That symbol felt too real; if they added that to all the other deceits, it would be too much.

"Did not, Dad."

"Did, too," he responded good-naturedly.

"Are you about done?" she asked, her hand rubbing at her back.

Calvin beat him to the answer. "Yep. I bet Peanut needs to get to sleep."

"Yes, she does. She's been kicking me to remind me that it's past bedtime."

It felt so natural for him to follow his son and wife to his truck. To drive home and recount the fun night. It felt even more natural when he rubbed Olympia's back.

"Calvin asked me something odd tonight," he said as Olympia wiggled into a more comfortable position in bed. The question of the ring had been nagging at him.

"Yeah?" she said, her voice drowsy.

"He asked why we didn't have rings." He immediately felt her stiffen. "I should have thought of it when we got married."

"Maybe," she said slowly, then her voice shifted to a pitiful sigh. "It wouldn't matter anyway. My fingers are sausages. Everything is swollen. I feel like a big water balloon. I thought with summer over, it would get better."

"It's still hot."

"The air-conditioning keeps it cool in here."

Was that an invite? He stopped rubbing her back, his hand slipping up to rest on her breast. Usually, he only did that when she made a clear invitation, but her declaration had been an invite of sorts.

She wriggled against him, her soft behind nestling against his crotch. "Hmm. Seems like something else is swollen."

He pushed his face into her fragrant nape, inhaling deeply the smell of French fries, salsa and Olympia. "I don't think the cool weather will make any difference."

"Anything I can do to help?" She moved slowly and suggestively.

He groaned and squeezed her breast, which wrung a soft moan from her. "These seem a little swollen, too." He kissed her neck and worked at lifting her nightgown. She gasped as his hand slipped between her thighs.

"I guess you forgive me."

For just a second, she stopped, then she said, "Maybe, but I won't forgive you if you don't finish what you started."

"Me?"

"Shut up and get about your business, cowboy."

"Yes, ma'am. Your pleasure is my command," he said in his best drawl.

Chapter Thirteen

Spence looked at his ex-wife, sitting at the other table in family court. Why had he thought her model good looks were beautiful? Probably the fact that they'd both been young, along with his desire to be part of Missy's large, interconnected, long-time Arizona family. But they weren't like he'd imagined. On the outside they were the Waltons, but once he'd gotten to know them, they were *The Real Housewives* meets *Duck Dynasty*. Spence's attorney poked him. Crap. Had the judge said something? Spence looked up and acted interested. If he could just stop going over the prenup again and again, looking for the loophole that would keep Olympia around... Then he'd tell himself he was an idiot. She didn't want to stay. Then he'd remembered their nights in bed and—

"Mr. MacCormack," the judge said, "your attorney says that your current wife has been integral in the raising of your son. Is there a reason she's not in court with you today?"

"She's pregnant, your honor."

"So you'll have another baby?"

Missy's attorney stood. "Your honor, we contend that

this new family will distract Mr. MacCormack and his wife from Calvin and his health needs."

"I was the one who slept at his bedside while he was sick, not Missy," Spence burst out, and stopped when his attorney yanked on his arm. He quieted immediately.

"We'll agree to the examiner, your honor," Spence heard his attorney say. What the hell had they just agreed to?

"Fine," the judge said, hammering down the gavel, "I'll make my decision after the visit from the agreed-upon examiner, who will determine the validity of the marriage and relationship between Mr. and Mrs. Mac-Cormack."

Spence's attorney dragged him out of court, refusing to answer questions until they were in the parking garage. He explained that Missy's attorney had accused Spence and Olympia of having a marriage of convenience in order to keep Calvin and the trust that had been set up for his son. So a trained psychologist/ social worker would determine the appropriateness of the home life as well as whether he and Olympia had a real marriage.

"Darn it, why did you agree to that?"

"Because you were stupid enough to file that damned prenup."

"We'll tear it up."

"It would still be on record. This is just a visit and some questions. Standard stuff... Sort of... I guess."

"Why am I paying for you again?"

"Because I'll get you custody of your son and access to his trust."

"I don't care about the money. I just want Calvin to

be raised right. Missy can't do it, and you see what a good job her folks did?"

"You said you and your wife are living together, thus creating a home, and that Calvin loves his stepmom. This is nothing."

It didn't feel like nothing to Spence, especially since some of those avowals might be stretching the truth. It felt like once again the future of his family was out of his control.

"AT LEAST IT'S not a surprise visit," Olympia said, looking around the disordered house.

"There is that." Calling the ranch house comfortable and homey was the polite way of saying out-of-date and rundown. It looked even shabbier with his what-will-someone-else-see goggles. On the plus side, all the appliances worked. But with his time limited and with Olympia so far along in her pregnancy that it made even dusting difficult, they'd soon need a shovel to deal with the mess.

"So what else besides the visit?"

"They want proof that we're a 'real' couple."

"I think we can do that. I'll call you honey."

"This is serious."

"I know. I'm sorry. We can do it, though. We've been doing it."

"I guess. Once we're through the visit and another court appearance, then Missy's family will stop hounding us. It's that darned trust."

"Trust?"

"There's a trust for Calvin. He'll get a portion of it at eighteen, then twenty-five, then thirty-five."

"Oh, my God, they don't care about him at all, do they? This is all about the money!"

"The money doesn't matter to Missy's parents as much as the control it represents. If I have full custody, they won't be able to use the funds to get Missy or even me to bow to their pressure."

"Why did you marry this woman? It sounds like a nightmare."

"It seemed like a good idea at the time."

"You mean you were thinking with your little cowboy—"

"Ha-ha," he said. Standing this close made him want her despite the seriousness of their discussion. If they were a real couple, he would have acted on what the "little cowboy" wanted. Even when he and Missy were newlyweds, he'd never had this ache to have her like he did Olympia. He wanted her no matter what. In the darkness of their bedroom, they were both able to forget that they were in the marriage for something other than love. He wanted to smooth his hands over her belly and then up to cup her spectacular breasts. She'd always been well-endowed, but now...well, her breasts were stars in a lot of his hot dreams.

She looked at him with a half smile, then turned away. "We've got to clean." She stepped aside and then pressed her hand hard against the side of her belly.

Cold fear snaked through him. Her paleness and the little furrow between her brows worried him. It was the same look she'd had before the last health scare. "What? Are you okay? Do I need to call the doctor?"

She drew in a deep, long breath. "No. It's those fake contractions. I'm fine. I just need to sit with my feet up for a few minutes, then I'll get working on the house.

I feel so bad that I didn't keep up. It's not as if I had anything else to do."

"Shh," Spence said, as he led her to their big bed. "Lie down on your side, like the doctor said, and relax. Calvin and I'll take care of things, and worse comes to worst, Lavonda and Jessie can come."

"Not Jessie. She hates cleaning," she said softly, curling around her belly, her forehead still creased. He didn't like that.

"If you feel worse, if you think that there are any problems, we can be at the hospital in twenty minutes."

"If we got there that fast, we'd be breaking the sound barrier," she said with a small smile.

"Rest." He just stopped himself from pushing the hair back from her face and kissing her forehead. He walked out of their bedroom, not sure what he should feel. He needed to focus on the next step in the custody case. That way, by the time the visit rolled around, he'd have it all under control.

As Olympia tried to stretch the kink out of her back, the court-appointed examiner settled himself on the recliner across from the couch where she and Spence had planted themselves. Why hadn't she let Lavonda help her get the house ready? Because she'd felt so darned useless lately, so she'd stubbornly insisted on doing the cleaning herself. The house would never be a show place, but it was tidy enough, even if she'd killed her back. She pushed her hand against Peanut, who somersaulted again and again.

"Mrs. MacCormack, I have a few standard questions," said the narrow-shouldered, pinched-mouth man, fingers poised over his laptop.

She nodded, and the man began to pepper both her and Spence with question after question. She tried to stay calm and keep in mind what they had gone over to make sure that their stories matched.

"I'm sorry," Olympia interrupted a long-winded question. "I need to use the…uh…well, you know." She rocked forward to get enough momentum to stand and hoped that she could waddle fast enough to the bathroom to prevent an accident. Spence gave her an encouraging smile. Or maybe it was a grimace because she was escaping the interrogation.

In the bathroom, she took extra minutes to calm her racing heart and give a pep talk to the round-faced, double-chinned woman in the mirror. Jeez. How had she gotten so huge? Water weight, right? Not that she was vain, but really, the puffer-fish look wasn't her favorite. Lifting her chin a bit helped.

She made herself open the door. She'd stalled long enough already. She walked with as much dignity as possible with her feet forced into ratty flip-flops. The examiner started in on her as soon as she sat down.

"So how many more children do you plan? And how will you balance that with your career as…?" He trailed off to let her respond.

How had she and Spence decided to answer questions about her career? She tried to glance at him from the corner of her eye without appearing to look toward him. "I'll be a stay-at-home mom." She stretched her face into a smile. She hoped it was a smile. From the pinch-faced man's reaction, she couldn't be sure.

"And more children?"

"Um, sure?" She pressed her hand against the whirling dervish of a baby. Dear Lord, would she really ever do this again?

"You're from a big family."

"Big?"

"I see from the paperwork that you have three siblings."

"That's not big."

"It's above average. Therefore, it is big."

Really. This was the guy they had to impress? A man who thought four children were too many for any one family. She opened her mouth to tell him that he needed to find a new dictionary when she heard a horsey snort from nearby. Like in the house. Shi…sheets. Could Lavonda have forgotten to close the pens this morning? A loud clop sounded from the kitchen. What the—?

"Limpy, Limpy," Cal said standing in the doorway to the kitchen.

"It sounds as if Cal needs me," Olympia said as she levered herself up, seeing in Cal's pale face a mixture of delight and…fear? She heard the distinct sound of a horseshoe striking linoleum and hurried faster. "Sheets," she said with feeling as she finally came into the kitchen to find Pasquale standing halfway through the open patio slider, his front quarters squarely in the room. His neck was stretched out, and his teeth were showing in a stupid grin that looked more threatening than it was. Cal had taught the horse that trick. The kid had talent. Why was he trying to show it off now?

Spence stormed into the kitchen and up to the horse, his tension rippling through her, too. "Calvin Leonard MacCormack, get this horse out of the house. What the hell do you think you're doing?" Spence stepped forward, and Olympia opened her mouth to remind him of Pasquale's protective streak. Too late. The horse's yellow teeth flashed out, grabbed Spence by the upper arm and bit down hard…if her husband's manly screech meant anything. Pasquale let go, shook his head and calmly backed up, turned and trotted across the yard to the barn.

"Pasquale and I wanted to show *that* guy our tricks," Cal said, pointing to the examiner who stood on the kitchen's threshold, "so he can see that I'm a cowboy and I need to stay here."

Olympia couldn't give in to the tears that sprang to her eyes. "I don't think Mr. Miller is a horseman," she said calmly. "Everything is just fine. Our horses are so well trained that they come to the house when their water buckets are empty. I'll take care of that after your visit." She waited until the examiner headed back to the living room. Then she leaned in and whispered to Cal. "Quick like a bunny, make sure Pasquale is in his stall with the latch on, then you can play on the computer in your room. Get your dad's laptop from the kitchen." The boy genius had just acted more like a boy than a genius. Why did it have to be today?

In the kitchen, Spence twisted his arm to see where Pasquale had grabbed him. No blood, thank goodness. "Do you need ice?" she asked softly. She didn't want any trouble from the man who'd decide the future of her family—dear Lord, her family? Was that how she really felt?

"What is it about me that makes your horses think I'm food?" he whispered at her, his brows drawn down in disapproval.

She shrugged and rubbed her hand over her belly,

trying to soothe the baby. "We'd better get back in there."

Spence reached out to grab her arm. "Olympia, we've got to impress this guy."

"I know. I'm trying. Don't you think we handled the parenting challenge of a horse in the kitchen well? I mean, I didn't kill Cal or yell at him. That has to get us points."

"Pretty low bar," Spence said as he followed her to the living room, where the examiner sat primly on the recliner.

"Mrs. MacCormack, how do you handle disciplinary situations like this?"

A pain shot from Olympia's back to her belly button as she tried to sit. She forced a smile. The pain had to be a fake contraction from the tension and strain of cleaning the house. "Well, sir," she started when she finally settled into her seat, rubbing her belly to ease the lingering ache, "Spence and I work together to ensure that our discipline is both fair and firm."

He typed into his laptop much longer than Olympia thought it should take for her answer. "How do you plan to ensure that Calvin maintains a relationship with his birth mother?"

Olympia felt Spence's anxiety. "We plan to keep an open line of communication with his biological mother and work with Cal on determining the level of engagement that suits his emotional maturity." Whew. She and Spence had talked about the answer for that question. Another twinge moved from her back to her belly. She rubbed at it absently.

"Sweetie," Spence said, his tone taut. "Are you okay?"

She immediately stopped rubbing her stomach and

sat up a bit straighter. "Sorry. The baby…" She trailed off. The inquiry had gone on for more than an hour.

"Not many more questions, Mrs. MacCormack," the examiner said, tapping on the laptop again. Then his head lifted and he sniffed the air, his nose twitching. "What is that smell? Is there another problem in the kitchen?"

Olympia took a deep breath—as deep as she could—and nearly choked. Spence's perfectly straight nose wrinkled in disgust. "I'm not sure," Olympia answered calmly, but then she heard it. Cal's whisper and a cut-off squeal. She forced herself from the chair. "Excuse me. It sounds like Cal might need some help in the kitchen," she said, and added, "No need for you to come out, honey." She'd identified the smell. It had been years, but it wasn't a stink that anyone would forget.

"Shh, Petunia," she heard Cal's little-boy whisper as she entered the kitchen. And there it was: a javelina, which right now was earning its "skunk pig" nickname. A small one, thank God, but the stench was overpowering. Nausea raced up her throat, but she fought it down. She had to get Cal and the smelly wild animal out of the house before Mr. Judgmental saw them.

"Out. What are you thinking?" She came closer, holding her hand over her nose and pointing to the back door.

"Limpy, she's hurt. Pasquale kicked her." Cal looked up, his blue eyes gleaming with tears.

"I'm sure she's fine."

"I think her leg is broken." The javelina struggled in Cal's grip and let out a little squeal before he could force her snout under his arm to quiet her.

"Sweetie," Spence called from the living room. "Everything okay?"

"Just a second," she called back. To Cal she said, "You know how important this is to your dad…and to me. Just a little more time, then I'll help you with the javelina. You need to take her back outside. She's a wild animal. I'm sure her mama's looking for her."

"I don't think so, or why would she have been in the barn? Pasquale's very sorry."

"I'm sure he is, but we can't have the javelina in the house. She stinks."

"I know, but her leg…" Cal said, and now Olympia could see what he meant. There was definitely something wrong.

Olympia felt bad for the little thing, which had a certain babyish cuteness, despite the odor. She pressed her hand to her own baby, who chose that moment for a powerful kick that rattled her kidneys and made her back ache. "She'll be fine if you put her on the patio." Cal shook his head, his blond hair flying.

"She needs the emergency vet."

Olympia closed her eyes to gather enough patience and strength to calm the baby and to get Cal to cooperate.

"What the heck are you two doing out here?" Spence asked in a low whisper.

Olympia's eyes popped open. She hadn't heard him come in. Cal squeaked, and the little animal squealed and scrambled from his arms, hopping along the floor, holding its front leg at an odd angle.

"Dad," Cal started as she hissed, "Spence, hush."

The stench increased, and Olympia's nausea went from DEFCON 4 to 2.

"Take that animal outside before we asphyxiate," Spence said.

"Excuse me," the examiner said, joining Spence in the doorway. "What is that?" He pointed to the little animal.

"A javelina," Cal said. "Her name is Petunia."

"First a dangerous horse, and now you have allowed your son to bring a wild pig into the house? With his health issues?"

"I just found her in the barn. Pasquale was mad because he couldn't stay in the kitchen for his snack and stomped on Petunia. Her leg is broken." Cal scrambled along the floor as he tried to catch the hopping pig-like creature, who beelined for the examiner, looked up, grunted, let go another cloud of stink and peed on his shoes. "Petunia didn't mean to," Cal said. "Don't paddle her ass."

Spence and Olympia gasped together as they looked from Cal to the man who had their future in his hands. His face screwed up in distaste. "I've seen *and* heard enough."

Spence followed the man from the kitchen. Olympia leaned against the wall, hoping her legs would hold her. "Oh, Cal."

"Petunia didn't mean to pee on his shoes."

"Why would you say that about paddling?"

He dropped his head as he cradled the smelly animal, who seemed to be sleeping now. "It's what Roger said his stepmom says whenever he does something bad."

Olympia saw his lip trembling and knew the boy felt awful. None of it would make any difference now. They'd have to hope that Spence's attorney found a good explanation, or they were all toast.

"Let's call my sister in Arkansas," she said to the boy. "She works as a vet tech. I bet she'll know what to do for Petunia."

SPENCE LISTENED TO his attorney sputter and bluster on the phone as he drummed his fingers on his office desk. He didn't need the other man to let him know that the examiner's visit had been a disaster. He'd lived it. Worse, the damned pig now resided in a box that Olympia and Lavonda had rigged up on the patio, stinking up the outside.

"I've got to go," he cut off his attorney in mid-diatribe. "I'm up to my neck in work. Do what you can. I can get character witnesses, whatever. Email me. Bye."

Talking about that disastrous visit gave Spence indigestion. He opened his bottom drawer, searching for a TUMS, Maalox, anything to put out the fire.

Should he call Missy and try to reason with her? Really, her parents were driving the court case. He discovered a roll of TUMS at the back of the drawer and chewed three of them. Could this be sympathy heartburn? That was what Olympia told him when he complained. She said that he needed to be quiet because she had the real thing; his was just pretend.

They'd been getting along fine, despite the stress, especially at night. Except the past few nights when she'd been too restless to sleep, staying up to watch rodeo reruns. He'd found her asleep on the recliner, her hand protectively cupped over her belly, early this morning. She also said that she had to stay in the living room because it was close to the kitchen and the door that led onto the patio where the little javelina resided. According to Calvin, who'd looked up the animal, the stench was from fear, and Petunia wasn't a pig but a peccary. Spence had told his son that there was no way she was afraid. She had a cozy box, plus food and clean bedding. The local rehab center wouldn't take her to be released into the wild until the broken leg healed—which to set had cost seven hundred and fifty dollars he didn't have. He'd have to find more money for his attorney somewhere, because this would be a fight. Maybe letters of support from his brother and Jessie would help. The men and women from the Hope's Ride program would give him good references, along with at least two other attorneys in the firm. He hoped that the court didn't dig too deeply into Olympia's family. If they did, they were sunk.

Where would they find next semester's tuition for Rickie and the money for animal feed? He'd thought once he got Calvin through surgery, then everything else would be smooth sailing.

His personal cell buzzed. Thank God. He needed the distraction. "Yes."

"Hello to you, too," Olympia said. Her voice sounded unstrained and light. "I've been thinking about that visit with Ferret Face."

"With who?"

"That examiner. Anyway," she said, dragging out the word, "we need to send letters or testimonies to the judge."

"Great minds think alike. I had just decided that we should contact Jessie and her crew. Get them to write letters. That's how they saved Hope's Ride."

"Do you think we have time?"

"Yes."

"Are you okay? You sound queasy."

"Just my stomach."

"I swear, man…do you have TUMS? Or Pepto?"

"It's just this visit. It might've been okay. But Petunia."

"Peeing on the guy was not her finest moment."

"That pig doesn't have any finest moments."

"Come on, she's pretty darned cute."

"Not you, too? She's not staying. She's a wild animal… who stinks."

"I know. I can smell her, and I'm in the living room. Dang. Cal," she yelled, "put Petunia in her cage. That's it. I've got to go and make sure he puts her back. We're not supposed to get her too used to humans or they won't be able to release her."

"Go," Spence said. He couldn't decide if the new churning he felt was more sympathy heartburn or that twisted, couldn't-put-a-name-to-it feeling that he got every time he looked at Olympia.

"See you at dinner. Bye. Cal…"

He stared at the phone and stopped himself from thumping his head on his desk. He was going crazy. He knew that she'd be leaving soon. His heartburn crept up his throat, making his eyes water. She had her own dreams and own life. He'd agreed to that. He didn't get to change the rules now.

Chapter Fourteen

Spence held his breath as he walked onto the patio, until he saw that Petunia was asleep. Thank God. No stench. Olympia made her way through the door behind him. She might complain that she was huge, but he liked—really liked—her rounded softness. He wanted her badly. He shifted, knowing his jeans couldn't hide what he felt and also knowing that just six weeks away from the birth, she wasn't up for anything other than cuddling.

"Petunia's finally settled," she said. "I thought I'd strangle Cal when he brought her into the house again. I've told him and told him—"

"He's a kid."

"He's a smart kid. I don't know what he was thinking."

"That he wanted to play with the pig. That's what he told me when I saw him digging in the yard. He said that you told him to make sure there weren't any weeds or no supper for him or Petunia."

"I didn't know how else to discipline him." The only sound on the patio was the little snore from Petunia followed by a soft snuffle. "Maybe Ferret Face is right to not recommend full custody while I'm in the picture."

"What?"

"I just said I wanted to strangle Cal."

"So? I think that ten times an hour when I'm home. He's a kid. I love him to death, but that boy can try the patience of three saints and a nun on Sundays, darlin'."

She didn't laugh. "Mama used to get mad like that."

Now he understood. She continued to insist she had no parenting instincts, which he just didn't get. He pulled her to him, rocking her a little bit, feeling the roundness of the new baby against his belly. "You're not like your mother. You have so much patience with Calvin. A lot more than Missy. More than I do some days."

"I…I don't want to be barefoot and pregnant, reliant on some man to pay the bills. That's what Mama always said we'd be."

"You're not. You have very nice boots on your feet, and your sisters—not one of them is pregnant or barefoot or—"

She sighed, laid her head on his shoulder. "I can't wear the darned boots. My feet are too swollen."

He couldn't stop himself from looking down at her pudgy feet in the dollar-store flip-flops. She kept her head lowered. "I'm so scared, Spence," she whispered, and he heard tears in her voice.

"I am, too. What do I know about raising a girl? How can I handle two children? How will I ever beat Calvin at Hedgehog at Saguaro Sal's?"

He felt her body shake a little with laughter. He gave her one final squeeze, wishing that he knew how to give her more comfort.

MAMA WAS RIGHT. Men were just weird. Pasquale stuck his head out of the stall and shook it at her.

"You're weird, too," she told the sweet horse. What else could explain Spence's increased interest in her now that her pregnancy clothes were getting tight? Two stalls down, Muffin curled his lip at Olympia, his way of "suggesting" that she owed him butter-rum muffins.

The baby kicked her ribs. How could she get back in shape enough to care for the ranch? Plus, Rickie would need more help to pay for next year's tuition, too. Olympia scuffed along the cement floor to Muffin's stall. She tried to take her steps carefully since she couldn't see her feet and was forced to wear sandals. Cowgirls didn't wear sandals. Another reason that she'd never be doing this pregnancy thing again.

"Muffin, what am I going to do with you?" He snapped his teeth at Olympia, his usual greeting when she came without a treat. "Stop being such a diva. Look at Pasquale. He's happy with whatever life sends him. But you? You're in a nice clean barn, you've got grain and someone to groom you and you still complain. Who will take you on, Muffin?" The horse pulled at the wood of his stall, tearing off a long splinter. "Stop that." Olympia reached out and grabbed his halter. Muffin pulled her forward. Olympia felt herself falling.

"Limpy," Cal screamed, and skinny little boy arms grabbed at her. Olympia caught herself just before she landed on her butt on the floor. "Did you hurt Peanut?"

"No, we're okay. Thank you. You saved me." She gasped a little from fear and the bent-over position that pushed the baby against her lungs.

"Dad told me come out and tell you that 'you shouldn't be in the barn, that's why we pay someone.'"

"We don't pay Lavonda. I was just visiting with Pasquale and Muffin."

"I know. He doesn't understand. You know he wouldn't even let me get a fish. I bet you could talk him into letting me have a dog. Since you won't let me keep Petunia. I mean, you're married and everything."

Olympia heard the note of fear and anxiety in Cal's voice. Married. *Not for much longer*, said a mocking voice in her head. She told the voice to pipe down and said, "That doesn't mean that we always agree."

Cal's small hand reached out and touched her belly. "Limpy, don't make us leave. I love Peanut. I want her to be my sister for real. I'll teach her how to be quiet and clean up."

Olympia's chest felt crushed by the weight of her emotions. She brushed at Cal's flyaway hair. "Why would you think you're leaving?"

"Don't be mad," Cal whispered, pressing his face farther into her side, making Peanut move away. "I read the contract."

"What?"

"The one about being married."

Why did he have to be so smart? "Your dad and I... We're good."

"But, Limpy, it said—"

"I know what it said, but we changed our minds. Adults are allowed to do that. We're all going to live here like a family, just the way we've been doing." Why had she said that? She had to take it back right now.

"Are you sure? Rickie told me you always wanted to be a barrel racer, and if you don't get to do that, you'll be sad for the rest of your life."

"Hey," Spence said from the barn door. "What are you two doing? It's time for everyone to come in for their snacks."

"I was just visiting," Olympia said, staring at her husband. The father of her baby. Her hand went to her belly to still the somersaults there. Darn it. Had her lie to Cal been a lie? Or was it what she really wanted? But what if Rickie was right? She'd never been this wishy-washy before. She wanted to blame Peanut for using all her blood supply. She had to be honest, though. Other than her sisters' safety, nothing had ever been as important to her as Cal and Spence. "You two go in. I'll be in in a few minutes. I need to talk with Muffin. He's being a stinker."

Spence's gaze stayed on her for more uncomfortable seconds. "Don't be long. You need to rest. Remember what the doctor said."

"That I was pregnant and women have been giving birth for thousands of years."

"That you're supposed to take it easy."

She nodded and turned to Muffin, who had perfected the horsey stink eye. She just needed Spence and Cal to leave the barn, so she could have a good cry—which she hated—then she'd get herself back to "normal." She had to move on with her plan for when Peanut made her appearance. Any other option just wasn't an option, was it? But why had she told Cal differently?

OLYMPIA GOT OUT of bed to pee—again. She'd started restricting her liquids like a little kid, and she still had to get up once or twice a night, which didn't make it easy to fix her erratic sleep schedule. She stifled any groans or complaints so she didn't wake Spence. Except right now his side of the bed was empty. Had she been so restless that Spence had had to go in the spare room? She checked there. Empty. She checked on Cal to make sure that he hadn't had some kind of nighttime trouble. The kid slept with the covers over his head and a dinosaur night-light. She sniffed the air to make sure he hadn't smuggled the javelina into the room. Nope. Smelled just like little boy—burned sugar and damp dirt.

Was she hungry? she asked herself after her pit stop in the bathroom. No way. She'd scarfed down enough at dinner to fill up two ranch hands after a ten-hour day working cattle. A dim light came from the small nook off the kitchen where Spence had set up his laptop. When she'd gone to bed at 8:00 p.m., he'd been on the couch.

"Spence," she whispered as she put a hand on his shoulder. His head was resting on his small desk. "Spence, come on. Time to go to bed." He didn't stir. She leaned down impulsively and whispered into his ear, "Honey, you need to come to bed. I miss you."

He hummed an answer, and she snaked her hand around his chest. What was wrong with her? Big as a house, an exhausted man and only one thing on her mind. Well, it'd certainly help her get back to sleep. She stood up, taking a moment to get herself under control, then Spence's fingers grabbed her wrist at the same time he twisted in his seat and got her into his lap. She could feel that he might have been up for a little bit of mattress gymnastics, even though her ability to do gymnastics was severely limited.

He rubbed his stubbly cheek against her neck and she shivered in reaction. "What were you looking for? A little snack? I've heard that pregnant ladies are always hungry." His hand moved to the edge of the nightgown, lifting it. "Olympia, you are so beautiful and wonderful. How did I get so lucky?"

Olympia relaxed into his body. He shifted and she felt the hardness of him against her. *Oh, my...* She snuggled into him, not ready to stop savoring the relaxed warmth and pleasure of the closeness. She reached her arms around his neck to give him a full on-the-mouth kiss. She wanted him, loving her, taking her. "Let's go to bed," she said before she could think of the reasons why they shouldn't.

"I'm fine."

"But I'm not," she said, levering herself from his lap and holding out her hand. "You need to give the pregnant lady what she wants, or it could get ugly."

In the soft glow of the light from the stove feet away, she saw his lips turn up and his sweet dimple deepen. "Your wish is my command."

"Ha. That's not true, but I know when I ask you to get horizontal, you'll listen. So let's go."

"What a husband is forced to do." He laughed. She wasn't going to think about the fact that he wasn't *really* her husband because she needed this. Maybe Spence needed it, too.

Chapter Fifteen

Spence's stomach gurgled with acid as he and his lawyer sat waiting for his ex's attorney to show up. Calvin knew what they were doing today, and he'd been as nervous as Spence this morning. Only Olympia had been Madonna serene. Spooky calm. Thinking about her, though, distracted him. This morning she'd made love with him to relax him. She'd insisted. He'd been so relaxed that he'd taken her hard and fast. He squirmed in his seat until his attorney gave him the stare. Spence couldn't settle down, couldn't stop his foot from jiggling. How much longer?

A woman dressed in a cheap suit came hurrying from the side of the courtroom. She whispered to the judge. He nodded, looked at Spence, asked a question of the woman, then pinned Spence and his attorney with a stern I'm-the-judge-and-I'm-in-charge glare. Spence sat up straighter. Something had happened.

"We're going to recess for fifteen minutes. It seems, Mr. MacCormack, that your ex-wife wants to appear before the court. When she gets here, we'll continue."

"Judge, if I might—" Spence's attorney started, and the judge held up his hand.

"I want to see this settled, and I understand that this

may do it without a long drawn-out battle and testimony. Making the hearing less acrimonious is always good for the child. Fifteen minutes." The judge pounded his gavel.

THE BUZZING SOUND of his attorney's voice didn't penetrate the fog Spence was in. Missy's deal couldn't be real. His ex didn't do things like this. She and her parents worked to make sure that Spence's life sucked. No way would she—they—agree to give up full custody and alimony for the next two years while Missy went to rehab again and tried to get her life back together. At the end of that time, there would be another evaluation to divide the custody more equally, if Missy's counselor thought it was in the best interest of Missy and Calvin. He wanted to talk with Olympia.

"Spence," his attorney said sharply.

"It's not enough time. If Missy is willing to compromise like this, she'll give me more time."

"I thought you wanted to get this settled."

"If she's willing to go for two years, I bet we can get five."

"Spence." His ex-wife's voice startled him. She stood less than five feet away in the corridor outside the courtroom. "I know that I've not been a good mother to Calvin, especially with all his health stuff. But I tried. I am trying. I love him, but I don't know that I'm cut out to be a mother...full-time."

He closed his eyes. That was exactly what Olympia had been saying about herself. Then, in the next moment, she'd help Calvin make a fort out of the picnic table on the back patio and brought him s'mores ranchero—an awful mixture of animal crackers covered in marshmallow fluff, raspberry jam, chocolate and chili powder. The two of them gobbled them up. He wanted to lash out at Missy. Tell her how she'd hurt Calvin. He stared at her hard. Her eyes glistened with tears. He didn't want to believe that they were for Calvin. "Good thing at least one of us wants to be a full-time parent."

She flinched. "It is a good thing. I'm working on it, Spence. I really am. Maybe you can bring Calvin to visit, even when he doesn't have counseling with me. I didn't know that Mother and Daddy were still hounding you. I thought that when I went to rehab…" She took a moment to gather herself. "When I went last time and left Calvin with you, I thought they understood." She shifted on her well-heeled feet. "I'm not asking you to forgive me or even for Calvin to do that. I just want… The counseling is important. I don't want him to end up like me."

Spence stopped himself from saying more nasty words. Missy couldn't be anything but what she was. At least she'd finally admitted she had a problem and that she had a responsibility to make sure her son had a chance at happiness. Maybe her childhood hadn't been any easier than his. Could that be why they'd gotten together? Now it was finally time for the two of them to end it and think about what was best for each other as well as their child. Missy had started that. He needed to step up, too. He turned to his attorney. "Tell the judge that I agree to the terms. You and my ex in-laws' attorney can iron out the details."

Missy smiled at him shyly and mouthed, "Thank you" as a stern-looking man in a suit placed his hand on her shoulder. She turned and walked away.

Spence's shoulders relaxed. Calvin was safe. His son wasn't going anywhere. He needed to call Olympia and let her know.

"Ranchero Loco," Olympia answered on the first ring.

"Bad day?" Spence asked with a laugh. Everything would be fine. He had his son and a new baby about to make an appearance. Then he remembered that this meant Olympia was nearly on her way to her new life.

"If by bad you mean that a javelina got into the house 'by accident,' ate chilies and bananas, then barfed everywhere, then, yes, it was bad."

"Ugh," Spence said with feeling, glad he hadn't been home.

"Don't sound so relieved. There'll be plenty for you to clean up when you get here. So how did it go? Okay, right? You sound good. Quick. Tell me before Cal comes back."

He grinned again. "Two years. Missy said that she'd give me full custody for two years with limited visitation from her, no alimony, and at the end of the time, we'll renegotiate. By then Calvin will be old enough that a judge should be willing to listen to what he wants."

"Spence, that's fantastic. Cal will be so happy. He wouldn't admit it, but he was worried. He wouldn't even eat my new s'mores javelina."

"I don't blame him. I'll stop on the way home and get a cake to celebrate. What should I bring for dinner?"

They talked for another few minutes. He felt as if he'd just won his first court case. He actually whistled as he went through the grocery store, putting all kinds of junk food into the cart, the kind he always told Calvin he couldn't have. Not tonight. Tonight they'd celebrate. He got sparkling cider, too, since two-thirds of the household couldn't drink.

And suddenly, he didn't feel much like celebrating. In mere weeks the baby would be born and Olympia would leave them. What would he tell Calvin? "Sorry, son. You get to stay with good old dad who can't seem to keep a woman." Today, when he'd understood that he finally had his son, he still hadn't felt whole. That was when it'd hit him. His family wouldn't be complete without Olympia. And not just that—he felt more for her than companionship or friendship or whatever other BS they'd been telling themselves when they'd gotten as close as two people could in their big bed. Could he talk her into staying? Of course, she cared about him and Calvin, too. But could he live with her knowing that she didn't love him?

OLYMPIA KNEW HER smile was as big as Spence's, although he also seemed a little sad. What was that? But even Peanut seemed happy, her movements only causing mini twinges. Maybe her baby would be a champion bull rider. For a second Olympia's own happiness faltered. Would she be around when Peanut was old enough to decide on a career? Or was she like Missy and willing to give up her child? She'd think about that another time, she told herself forcefully. Tonight she'd help her guys celebrate. Spence finally had just what he wanted: a family.

"Limpy, Limpy." Cal's little-boy voice hit its top register. "Dad said that we'll go to Disneyland."

"Disneyland?" When had Spence decided that? They didn't have the money. But that wouldn't be her problem soon.

"Next summer," Spence said. "By then, the baby will be old enough, and Calvin will have saved enough money to pay his own way, right?"

Cal stared at his father in disbelief, and then the two of them had a good-natured argument. She watched, her heart hurting. Soon she'd be gone. What would they tell Cal? Could they stay a couple until he was old enough to really understand? How would Spence care for the new baby and work enough hours at the firm? To stay married, though, she'd be giving up on barrel racing. It would also mean being with Spence without *truly* being with him. He might want her in bed, but she knew that wasn't love. Her feelings for him wouldn't change, but could his? No. Every James woman knew that was just a fairy tale.

She caught a shift in the tone of the discussion when Spence said, with dimple showing, "Maybe Aunt Jessie and Uncle Payson will come with us, too. Your uncle just loooves to get on rides, especially ones that spin." She imagined never hearing that teasing tone again. She rubbed low on her belly. In the past half hour, Peanut had taken to kicking in one place, and that made her ache.

"No, he doesn't," Cal said, and the two of them began arguing again.

Olympia walked slowly to the kitchen. She'd thought pretending to be a couple—a family—would be no big deal. Even now that she had to admit she'd fallen for Spence, she was sure she could wall off her emotions. She'd done that for years, learned to keep her heart protected. But Spence kept putting cracks in that wall, messing with her ability to stay safe. Mama had loved all those men, and Grammy had always said that she'd had her heart broken by each of the men who'd left her with another baby. Why couldn't this be easy?

"Another toast," Spence said as she made her way back from the kitchen. "Come on, Olympia, we're going to drink to making Uncle Payson snort soda through his nose when Calvin ambushes him and tickles him until he surrenders."

"That's terrible. Why would you do that to your brother?" Olympia's chest squeezed. She clenched her fists to stop the tears. She wanted to tell him how she felt, but she was sure that his love for her was only for what they did in the bedroom. She did want to stay here and raise their children. She wanted to be in his bed every night, telling him what had happened during the day and listening to him tell her about his cases. But was that the way it would be? Or would it be like her mama? Alone with the babies and all the responsibility. *You won't ever be alone.* Olympia clearly heard that voice in her head. Her breath stopped in her chest again as a pain lanced low in her belly. *Never.* It wouldn't be just her against the world. It would be them. Even if Spence didn't love her, he wouldn't abandon them, because they were his family. He wasn't the kind of man who walked away. He believed in family, believed in sacrificing everything to create that family. She'd done the same thing but called it something different. She'd fooled herself all these years.

"Olympia," Spence asked, near to her. His tone was worried and…she couldn't tell what else because her center was crumbling, that place she'd built to protect herself from the pain of disappointment and rejection. Now she wanted to run toward all that scariness.

"Olympia, talk to me. Is it the baby?"

"What?" she asked, only then realizing why she couldn't breathe. She was hunched over. She tried to straighten, and a pain lanced up her inner thigh to rest in a throbbing ache just to the right of her hip bone. She pushed there and felt the baby kick hard.

When had she sat down on the kitchen chair? Cal patted her arm, and in the background, Spence talked with someone loudly. Why did he sound so upset? Had Cal's mom changed her mind already?

"Olympia, look at me," Spence shouted inches from her.

She pulled her head up slowly and focused on him, wondering vaguely why he thought she couldn't hear him. The lines between his brows had deepened and his usually lush mouth stretched into a thin, taut line. She needed his help to figure this all out. He'd know what to do. "How could I have been so wrong? How can I stay safe?" She needed to answer that question now. Because being that vulnerable scared the crap out of her. Jeez. Her back hurt.

Spence's long fingered hands were on each side of her face, making her look at him. "How long have you been having contractions?"

"Contractions? No. Peanut's kicking, and I twisted wrong. That's why my—" She had to stop as the pain shot through her back.

"Think. When was the first pain?"

Another electric zing started low in her belly and wrapped around to her back. She hunched over again. "Ouch." She heard her voice, but it came from far away. *Crap.* Peanut wanted out. *Not now.* Olympia needed more time. She really, really needed to make Spence understand she was staying.

"Olympia, we're getting in the truck. Payson says I need to get you to the hospital."

"No. It's not time."

His hand shook where it covered hers on her belly. "The baby didn't get the memo."

She looked at Spence, whose face was white. What did he mean the baby was coming? "We have weeks. I have weeks to get ready. I don't have diapers."

"Not anymore... I don't think... Come on, we've got to go. Calvin, help me." She felt herself being pulled to her feet and shuffled along. Then another pain started low and hard. She panted as she tried to rise above it, but the pain dragged her down, made her think that she'd never feel anything else. Then it was gone. She was in the truck, buckled in, with Cal's little hand patting her shoulder.

"Olympia, honey...breathe, remember? The moaning... it's... Breathe, that'll help," Spence said, his voice low and strained.

"Hmm... Moan... I wasn't moaning. Cowgirls don't moan."

"Breathe," Spence said, glancing over at her. "Isn't that what you're supposed to do?"

"I'm not having the baby yet."

"That's not how it works." Spence grasped her hand. "You'll be fine. The baby will be fine. It's not really early. Calvin came even earlier, and look at him."

"Yeah, Limpy, look at me. Peanut will be fine. Dad said that Mommy thought she'd eaten a bad chile rellenos, then there I was."

"Yep. Just like that."

Olympia shook her head. She needed just a little more time to work things out. "They're going to send me home and tell me to put my feet up and have you guys wait on me." She ground together her back teeth, refusing to get pulled under by the pain.

"We already do that." Spence's grin didn't show off his dimple, and the line between his brows hadn't gone away.

"It's probably those new s'mores that Cal and I invented. Just indigestion."

"It's okay, Limpy. Dad and I will be there, and we'll make sure that you and Peanut are okay. The needles aren't so bad. Just don't look when they put them in. That's what I did." He patted her shoulder again, and his sweet breath wafted over her cheek.

"You need to get back in your seat belt," she said automatically—just like a mom. Dear Lord. What was she doing? She pressed against the headrest, bracing for the next contraction and for the wave of love that hit her thinking of the Peanut in her arms. Her baby. How could she ever have thought she'd walk away from their baby? "If anything happens," she said urgently but softly so only Spence could hear, "you'll make sure Peanut is okay. Right?"

"Nothing will happen. Missy said the same thing. The books—"

"Promise me. I know what I said all along about the baby, about…well, everything." The pain swelled, but she forced the air out to finish her sentence. "But really, I want to have a family. I want to be a family. I don't know how it works, though—"

"Of course we'll always be family." Spence's hand covered hers and pressed as the pain wrapped around her again. This couldn't be right. There was supposed to be space between contractions. Time when it didn't hurt.

"Limpy, you're our family, just like Peanut and Petunia and Pasquale and even Muffin. Remember, I drew the picture and explained. No matter what happens, you'll always be family. Like Mommy isn't always at the house or Uncle Pay or Aunt Vonda, but they're still family. Right, Dad? Just pick up the phone and call, and family is there. That's what it means, Limpy."

Chapter Sixteen

Spence couldn't stop staring at his new daughter—Audie Sage James MacCormack. Swaddled tight in her blanket, the baby looked tuckered out after making an early appearance—but not too early, the doctor said. As much as he wanted to just stand and stare, it was time for Olympia to see her daughter and know that she was perfect. He heard the change in the tenor of conversation among the nurses and doctor. He didn't hear Olympia.

"Mr. MacCormack." A nurse stepped into his space. "We need you to sign this." Another brightly dressed nurse plucked the baby from him.

He watched his daughter get settled in the bassinet, until his attention was caught by the huddle of personnel around Olympia. "What's wrong?" He tried to move past the nurse. She stepped in front of him.

"You need to sign this."

"What is it? What's wrong?" he repeated.

"Spence?" Rickie asked from the doorway to the room, holding Calvin's hand. She'd gone to get drinks for them.

The doctor's voice roared above the noise in Spence's head. "We've got to go now. Call the OR."

His heart stopped. Audie let out a squeak. The nurse

led him into the hall, where Rickie started to cry. He looked between her and the nurse with the paper. "What's going on?"

"Your wife is bleeding. We may need to do a hysterectomy to stop it."

He gasped.

"Postpartum hemorrhage. Serious but treatable," Payson said, his clear and clinical voice steadying Spence.

"Yes," the nurse said. "We need the permission. There isn't time—"

"Spence," Payson said. "It's probably nothing. Just placenta that didn't deliver or a little tear. They're just using the OR as a precaution."

"But she wants me to sign—"

"That's to cover their butts from lawyers like you," Payson joked. Spence didn't laugh.

"She couldn't have any more babies," Spence whispered.

"It's the worst-case scenario. That's what we docs do."

Spence searched his brother's face for the truth. "But it could happen. Don't lie."

"It's not likely."

"Sir," the nurse said. "We need the permission now. They're prepping her."

"Why the hell can't she sign this? She should be signing this," he said, his voice rising.

"Daddy, what's wrong? You swore. Can I see Limpy?"

"She… They…"

"Move," the normally placid Dr. Neiman shouted as she pushed Olympia's bed through the door. Spence stared at his too-still wife, her face as pale as skim milk and her eyes closed.

He ran after the bed, ignoring the nurse who spoke to him as she tugged at his arm. Doors thudded open and he didn't slow down.

"Spence, get back to the waiting room," Dr. Neiman yelled at him. "We're going to the OR."

"Not until I talk with Olympia."

"There's no time," the doctor said, standing guard outside the doors to the brightly lit operating room. "She's bleeding, and I've got to stop it."

"I can't sign this. She would never forgive me for not talking to her. How can I make a decision like this for her?"

Spence was desperate. He had to see Olympia. He had to tell her to hang on, tell her that he loved her. Dear Lord. Why hadn't he told her before? He couldn't let her go into surgery without her knowing. What if this was—?

The doctor's voice sharpened as she said, "You have as long as it takes me to scrub in and the anesthesiologist to get here. Suit him up."

"Olympia," he said through the mask.

"Don't touch anything," the nurse told him sternly.

Olympia's arms were strapped onto boards. Tears streaked her face. "Olympia," he whispered. "Everything's fine. Payson said it's just a precaution. He's sure. Maybe a few stitches. Do you understand?" Her eyelids moved up slowly and her gaze took a moment to land on him.

"Peanut?"

"She's fine. Her uncle is with her."

Olympia licked her lips. "As long as Peanut is okay, that's fine." Her eyes closed again. "Whatever happens to me doesn't matter."

"The hell it doesn't matter." He knelt beside Olympia's head and stroked her cheek. Her tabby-cat eyes opening enough that he could see her fatigue and something that frightened him. "Olympia, Audie needs you. Calvin needs you…I need you. If anything happens to you…" He swallowed hard. "Sweetheart…darlin'… without you, there is no family. There's no happiness for me. You're my cowgirl, my brave, fearless, lovely… Oh, God, Olympia, you can't—"

OLYMPIA'S EYELIDS WEIGHED a ton. She forced them to stay open, to keep her gaze locked on Spence's. She wanted him to understand. "Don't plan to go to the big rodeo in the sky," she tried to joke, but her mouth was so dry that the words came out cracked and weak.

"Could've fooled me."

"I'm not." But her head felt disconnected from her body. "I have a lot to stick around for. Peanut. Cal. You." She put everything into those few inadequate words, the ones she'd been holding back. "The horses, too. Got to get Muffin sorted out."

"Shut up about the damned horse."

"Swearing," she whispered automatically, and thought she smiled.

At the corner of her vision, she saw Dr. Neiman looking angrily at Spence. "Thirty seconds. Sign the damned paper."

"No. I—" Spence looked haunted.

"What?" she asked, working hard to keep him in focus.

"They need permission for the surgery."

"Surgery?" She tried to lick her lips. Everything felt numb.

"It's probably nothing serious." She heard his hesitation, and the noise of the nurses and machines faded. "They may need to do a hysterectomy. I couldn't... I just couldn't make that decision for you. They said you couldn't sign because... You know those lawyers."

Her mouth was so dry. "Want to be around for you... our kids—"

He covered her lips with his fingers. "I love you. I don't care if there are no more babies. I don't care... I just want you."

Gathering her strength, she whispered fiercely, "I love you, Spencer David MacCormack." There. She'd said it. Everything would be fine. Admitting she loved him and accepting that her life had taken a huge left turn lifted a weight that she hadn't even known she'd been carrying around.

"Time," Dr. Neiman said. "Sign the paper."

Olympia saw a clipboard come at Spence. He signed with a shaking pen. "I love you," he said again, as if he couldn't repeat it often enough. That was fine with her. She wanted to hear it again and again.

BLINKING HURT, NOT as much as the tight pounding at his temples, and none of it mattered. Spence's wife and daughter were okay. No thanks to him. He rubbed his forehead, hoping that he could wipe away the pain as he paced outside Olympia's room. He thought he heard something and burst in.

"What?" Olympia croaked. She was on her feet, leaning against a nurse's arm.

"Are you okay?"

"Of course. After they did the exam, I wanted to go to the bathroom—"

"I could have helped you."

"You should go home and sleep."

"Not while you're still in the hospital. Who knows what trouble you'll get into or what you'll sign if I'm not here."

As the nurse settled Olympia on the bed, she said, "I'll be back in fifteen minutes with the baby. She's done with her treatment for today, and I'm sure she'll be hungry and wanting Mommy."

Spence didn't move. Olympia looked nearly as white as the sheets and dark circles ringed her eyes. She didn't look like a woman who could nurse and care for a baby—she looked as if she should still be in intensive care. He pulled out his phone, intending to call—

"Put that away," Olympia said with that steely voice she used on the horses.

"I'm calling Payson. Maybe he can talk to the doctors. You should still be in ICU."

"No."

"Have you looked in the mirror?"

"I'm just tired. Rebuilding blood takes time. If you'd let me eat pudding, it'd help."

"Don't joke."

"I know how bad it was, but I'm better now and so is Peanut."

"Audie," he corrected automatically. A smile stretched across Olympia's face. "It's obvious to me that neither you nor your doctors understand. Wait until they get my paperwork."

"Stop, Spence. Enough. I'm fine or will be. Jaundice

happens to a lot of babies. A little time under the light and she'll be fine."

He wanted to go to Olympia. He wanted to grab her and hug her, to make sure that she never went away, that nothing bad happened to her. But he'd already proved that he was piss-poor at keeping her safe. "Calvin nearly died from a heart condition, and I can barely scrape together the funds to pay for it—"

"Missy's parents would have—"

"He's my son. I take care of my own family. If I don't do that, then what am I?" God. He sounded so pathetic, so needy. He glanced at Olympia, expecting to see disgust and resentment on her face, the look that Missy had gotten when he'd told her that they couldn't afford something.

"Oh, Spence, come here," Olympia said, holding out her hand.

He saw it shaking, and his chest tightened. "I can't. I can't—"

His wife, the woman he loved—why had he waited so long to tell her? He'd almost lost her. If he had… Now he was letting her down. How was he going to live with his worry and failure?

"If you don't get your butt over here, I'm coming to you." Olympia sat up in bed.

He hurried over, easing her back down, tucking in the covers, wanting to keep her safe. "Stop. Don't you understand? You nearly died."

"I know. I was there. I remember you in the operating room, bullying your way in there before you'd sign anything. Dr. Neiman told me that she almost called security." Her mouth curved into a grin.

"I couldn't sign that paper. I had to—"

She reached up and grabbed his hand, her fingers chilly but strong. "I know Peanut and I scared you, but we're okay. Just like Cal's okay. You were the dad. The big, strong man of the house. You made sure your family was safe. You did a good job, Spence. You cowboyed up. You would do anything for the people you love."

She tugged on his hand, and he collapsed onto the edge of her bed, suddenly needing the solid warmth of her presence. "Not much of a job. I just stood there."

"I knew you were there. Peanut knows you're there. Sometimes that's all anyone needs. You can't fix everything, you know."

"God, don't I know it. If I'd been able to fix everything, Missy wouldn't need to be in rehab. Calvin wouldn't ever need another surgery, and Audie wouldn't be stuck under some damned bili light."

"But since you're not God…or even a doctor…maybe you need to focus on what you can do. You know, like sit here with me so I don't get bored. Go home and sleep so you can be awake with Cal and take care of Petunia, Pasquale and Muffin. All that stuff matters. Maybe more than the big stuff. That everyday stuff… You know, I'm beginning to think that's what really makes a parent. I hope so anyway, because that's about all I have going for me."

THE POSTPREGNANCY HORMONES were the only explanation Olympia could come up with for sounding like *Dr. Quinn, Medicine Woman*. She reached out and patted Spence's knee as he sat beside her, head down. The warm fuzzies in her chest fired up as she caught Spence's black-licorice scent. She recalled that aroma somewhere during the darkness that had overshadowed Peanut's birth. What she remembered with a clarity that would stay with her forever was when he'd said that he loved her. She smiled. The two of them were a mess, loving each other and keeping it to themselves. They'd had to wait until a surgical drama of soap-opera proportions to admit what everyone had known, if Lavonda and Jessie were to be believed.

"I almost lost you," Spence whispered, his voice hoarse. "What would I have done?"

Her poor man. "Go home and get sleep. You're just tired. You'll be back to large and in charge tomorrow." His hand convulsively tightened on hers.

"Don't joke. Don't freakin' joke about this. I can't… I don't…jeez." Like a horse who'd been ridden too long and hard, his head hung down, swaying from side to side, dazed, stunned, exhausted but wanting to go on. The stallion protecting his herd and keeping them safe.

"Spence, we're fine. We're all fine."

"For now."

"For now. That's all we can ever count on, isn't it? And for now I'm relaxed and sassy. Peanut is snoozing under a sun light, like the diva she'll be, and Cal is being spoiled by everyone. He's in pig heaven. Or maybe it's javelina heaven?" She watched his face closely and made a note of the tension in his body.

"What will Calvin do when we have to take the creature to the sanctuary? Huh? He'll be heartbroken."

"He and I talked about it. We decided we'll be sad for forty-six minutes, and then we'll be happy and talk about all the fun javelina stuff Petunia'll do with her friends. He's a smart kid. He knows that she's not a pet, that she belongs out in the desert. But I'll bet he'll use the whole I-miss-Petunia thing to lobby for a dog or a pony. Jessie said that she'd let us have Molly." She waited for Spence to say something or at least laugh. No one would take Molly from Jessie, even if the pony was a pain in the butt and needed more attention than six full-size horses. "That's it, Gloomy Gus." She tugged on his hand to get his attention. "I won't allow you to be all down on yourself or what you can do or how you handle anything. It's just ridiculous." She pushed herself up a little in the bed and regretted that. Having a baby was not for sissies.

"I'll call the nurse," Spence said, his finger hovering over the red button.

"I'm fine, just a little sore." He tried to stand, but she held his hand tight, twisting a little like she did to Muffin to keep that stubborn horse in line. "Don't move. We have to talk. I'd wanted to wait, but…well, I think we need to iron this out."

She saw his Adam's apple move as he swallowed. She wanted to kiss that neck and rub the tension out of his shoulders. "I know our agreement doesn't cover this." When she saw his mouth open, she pinched the back of his hand. "Listen to me, and stop saying stupid things. You know I didn't grow up in a real family." She tightened her hold again when he tried to open his mouth. "I told you to stop talking. I had to raise my sisters, more or less. There was never enough money or love. We were scared a lot of the time. I promised myself I'd never get caught in a situation like that when I grew up. Then I went to that darned wedding, and you really are very good at persuading people to your point of view.

And, here we are, with two kids, a ranch, horses and a marriage. We're kind of stuck together."

"Stuck? Some people would say that families love each other."

"Well, sticking it out is loving each other." Her heart fluttered as she groped for words and tried to ignore her sweating palms.

"You've said that you love me when…well, you know. Are you saying now it's only because there's no choice?"

Olympia looked at his face, at his dusty-blue eyes. The dark circles made her want to fold him in her arms, but the dimple that hid in his cheek made her want to kiss him silly. "What about you? You've probably been thinking with the little…you know—" She looked down at his lap.

"First, no man likes his pleasure machine referred to as *little*." That startled a laugh out of her. "I know we started out with a contract and an end-by date, but somewhere along the way, I just went and fell in love with you, darlin'. Just like I told you." He smiled sweetly at her. "I don't feel stuck. I feel free. Free because I know that you love me, right? You said it, and you can't take it back—even if some days you'll forget that—and I know I love you. We're a team, a pair. We're like Dale Evans and Roy Rogers."

He was right. That fluttery feeling was love and freedom. How could that be, when her whole life she'd run away from love and responsibility to get free? He laced his fingers through hers, his beloved face hollowing out more under his cheeks. He lifted her hand and kissed her knuckles, his eyes bright with tears, even under the crappy hospital lighting. She said, "Kiss me for real. I never got one when we said, 'I do.'" She saw his dimple just before his mouth locked on hers. Finally, she was free.

Chapter Seventeen

Four weeks. Olympia had been a mom for four weeks. Although Spence said that was wrong because she'd taken on Cal months ago and that counted. She had to agree. Her Cal-boy had wormed his way into her heart just like that darned Muffin, who was staying on with them despite his lack of manners and his unnatural love of butter-rum pastries. She heard Peanut's breathing change as the baby squirmed but didn't wake.

Spence paced as he talked on the phone with his brother. "Audie doesn't cry enough. I want you to fly here and check her out. Her pediatrician's an idiot."

He looked hot. Just thinking about sex should have been impossible, considering what had happened a month ago and that she walked around the house like a zombie half of the time because she got so little sleep. Still, the sight of Spence sleeping beside her, the surprisingly dark lashes against his lean cheeks, just made her heart sing and her other places happy, too. Olympia ignored Spence and went back to the paperwork. Soon she'd be Cal's legal guardian, responsible for him in a more than an I-married-your-dad way. Olympia couldn't adopt Cal outright, but this was close. Her hand trembled a little as she signed her name. Yep. She hadn't wanted to be a mom. Hadn't wanted anything but the rodeo. Now—

"Damn it," Spence said with heat and just a hint of fear.

Olympia tensed. Her mothering hormones—or whatever they were—told her whoever was on the other end of the line was going to get an earful. Peanut writhed, also tuned in to her daddy's every mood.

Olympia watched him closely as she rocked Peanut back into sleep. Spence paced tight loops in their small, packed-with-baby-stuff bedroom. On his next loop, Olympia got a good view of his face. She immediately gathered herself and Peanut, stood and walked to him. Something really, really bad had happened. Obviously, he wasn't still on the phone with his brother. Whoever was on the other end of the call had upset Spence. More than upset. The man quivered with anger. She reached out and touched his arm. The muscles under her hand were ironwood hard.

"I know my attorney gave you my proposal. I'm not discussing anything beyond that. Thank you for letting me know that Missy is doing well. I'll take Calvin to see her when *I* think it's appropriate. Now I've got to go." He slammed the phone down on the dresser and Peanut jumped against Olympia's shoulder.

"Shh, baby. Just Daddy being noisy."

"I'm going to get a lot louder." Spence stomped out of the room.

Well, hell, Olympia thought, absently patting the baby's back. Worse than bad. Epic disaster. What had Missy's parents done now?

Twenty minutes later, Olympia adjusted the sling that held Peanut against her but kept her hands free.

She took a deep breath before walking into the barn. Despite not growing up a cowboy, Spence'd become competent—more than competent—at caring for the animals. Fortunately, they were down to two horses and one javelina. Petunia needed to go to the animal sanctuary, but Olympia had been too busy to enforce the pact she and Cal had made when they'd taken on the animal's care.

Olympia heard Muffin's distinctive growling grumble. "Hush up. I didn't get to the store, so I don't have any muffins," Spence said in a no-nonsense voice. Olympia opened her mouth to call to her husband when he went on. "Shi…crap, what am I going to do? They're at it again. Move over so I can put hay in here."

She heard Muffin snort and the shift of his hooves through the drifts of straw. The horse hadn't bitten Spence. He did have a magic touch. Maybe he was more cowboy than he knew.

"Biting them might seem like a good idea, Muffin, my man. I'd love to take a huge chunk out of Missy's parents. The two of them totally messed up their daughter. I'm not letting them get their cold, greedy hands on Calvin. But if the court sends another examiner out here, what's he going to say?"

Muffin gave a sympathetic, wet sigh. Olympia's chest squeezed with worry. Not Cal. Not this all over again. They had just gotten themselves settled into something that felt like a family.

"The stable is cleaner and more organized than the house. How can one small baby make such a mess? We're talking a mess like Hercules faced in that stable." A snort answered him. "Sorry, pal, I didn't mean you. You are a very clean horse. Thanks for keeping it to one corner. Are you sure you're not part dog? Move your head and I'll get the other side. Gotta look good for the ladies. Though I guess you're lacking in what the ladies really want."

Should she step in now? What would she say? That everything would be all right? They both knew it was a lie. With Missy's parents involved, deep pockets could prevail.

"They've got a case, Muffin. Honestly. I checked before the call. Grandparental rights are a thing. Courts have been more open to that, and with Missy still in rehab... Da...darn it. I can see a judge at least listening to them. They've got money for tutors, for more therapy." The mixture of human male and horsey sigh hurt her. Peanut stirred, disturbed by the noise, and let out a little squeak of annoyance.

"Calvin?" Spence asked.

Olympia froze. Stay or go? This was family stuff, and family worked it out. "It's me, Spence."

"What are you doing out here?" Spence leaned out from Muffin's stall. Then the horse's head appeared beside him.

Crap. Annoyed Muffin equaled biting Muffin. "Spence, move slowly, very slowly to the side."

"Huh?" He pushed the horse's head out of the way and Muffin moved without taking any of Spence's very capable fingers with him. When had her husband turned into a real cowboy? She was the one with the horse talent, but here she stood frozen, afraid of the horse that he so casually batted away.

"Nothing," Olympia finally said. "I wanted... So what are we going to do?"

"*I'm* going to finish cleaning up out here, even that darned pig. *You* are going back in the house and rest."

"I'm fine. But what's up with Missy's parents?"

"You heard at least part of it. They're back to suing for full custody because of a 'chaotic household and the need for his biological mother to have greater access to her son as part of her ongoing rehabilitation and therapy.' What crap. They just want everyone in their set to look at them as saints…martyrs…whatever. They're probably angling for exposure on *Good Morning America*. There's the trust fund, too—"

"Chaotic? That's not true."

"Out of all that, that's what you're worried about?"

"No one likes to be called incompetent, and that's what they're saying. Sure, the house is a little messy, but we just had a baby."

"I don't remember it being so bad with Calvin."

"That's because you didn't have another child. Cal has found his inner boy." Flutters started in Olympia's middle when Spence smiled and his dimple sprang into life. She was a mom, with her baby hanging around her neck; she shouldn't be thinking naughty thoughts.

"He is getting to be all boy, isn't he? I'm getting him cowboy boots and a hat for his birthday. It's a couple months away, but he'll love them. I also think this summer we should send him for a few weeks with his aunt and uncle, maybe after Disneyland. He'd love to help at Hope's Ride. It would give him a chance to learn more about riding, and helping other kids would be good for him."

"Will this be settled by summer?"

Spence tensed, and Muffin rubbed his shoulder in sympathy. "One way or another. It's just that I already have a huge bill with the attorney, and this isn't going to be cheap."

"We'll find the money."

"I'll just have to take the case back."

"But you said that an attorney who has himself as a client is a fool, or something like that."

"That's true when you actually have money to pay for an attorney."

Peanut wiggled again, her previously periodic movements working up to a full-blown squirm, which would be followed by yelling or even a full-out tantrum. How did kids learn that so early?

"Maybe the baby and I need to go to my sister's in Arkansas. Jolene lives on a farm there. She's the chicken whisperer or something. She would have me for a little bit. She's not much on babies, but I could talk her into it. I'd find places for the horses and Petunia. It would make it simpler, and you'd be able to rent a place right in Tucson that doesn't have leaking toilets or appliances that should be in the Smithsonian. Then you could concentrate on the case."

"I know you're an intelligent woman, but sometimes you can be so dumb," Spence said, sidling out of Muffin's stall. He planted himself in front of her, smelling of horse and licorice. Olympia inhaled deeply. Peanut settled back into the sling with a big sigh. "I know it's not what you wanted or planned for, but we're family."

Olympia's muscles relaxed, and she could take a deep breath. The baby hummed in contentment. "I know, but Cal was your family first—"

Spence reached out a hand, and Olympia didn't move away as he pulled her and the baby close. The three of them stood there for a moment. She soaked in the warmth, the reassurance of the contact. Then Spence spoke. "I know you're skittish about this family business. You sacrificed so much for your sisters, but maybe it wasn't a sacrifice. You helped each of them to move on, and they're all doing fine because you worked together as a family."

"But what about Mama and Grammy and all the other James women?"

"The James women have done what they had to do to survive. That's what your mama did. Maybe she didn't make the best decisions, but she kept you girls together," he plowed on. "Your mama and what she should have done is a discussion for another time. Right now I need to know that you aren't going to run away to your sister's, because I can face anything as long as I know you're standing with me."

"It would easier and better without Audie and me here to mess things up."

"That's family. It's messy. At least, I hope, it is, because the perfect house and the perfect-looking kids didn't do much for Payson and me, and certainly didn't help Missy."

"That's not—"

"We get to decide what family is, and this is working well for us. For the first time in his life, Calvin is acting like a little boy, and Audie is growing like a weed. What more could we want? Didn't someone say, 'Life is what happens to you while you're busy making other plans'?"

Olympia let Spence rock her and the baby. She'd had plans to follow the rodeo, to be footloose and fancy-free, one of those cowgirls the country-and-western singers crooned about. That had been the plan, but now? She didn't think so. There was Peanut and Cal, these danged useless horses and the broken-down ranch. And Spence.

He stopped moving and held her a little way from him so that his dusty-blue gaze locked with hers. "So what do you say, Mrs. MacCormack? Should we make this official?"

"Official?" she asked, dazed by the heat and love in his gaze. Maybe home wasn't such a boring place. Maybe being a family wasn't about crushing responsibility, but having that place that gives you refuge so you can go out and fight the good fight.

"I had this all planned out, but you know the plans of mice and MacCormack men." Spence dug in his pocket and held out a small box. "Here."

"What's this? We can't afford this." She wrapped her arms around Peanut. She knew in that little box was the ring they'd never gotten in Las Vegas.

"We have to afford it because this marriage is legit. Without a ring, it isn't."

"You're taking advice from a seven-year-old who thinks the only way to prove you're married is a ring?"

"When he's right, he's right. There's one for me, too. I'm good with having a quickie wedding in Vegas with Elvis, but I want the rings. Guess I'm just an old-fashioned, romantic cowboy." The hint of a dimple showed, then his face settled into sterner lines. "We are ripping up that prenup, too, because family isn't created by a court or a signature. What are you thinking about?" Spence asked nervously. "You kind of look like Muffin, right before he tries to bite off my fingers or—"

She grabbed him and kissed him hard on the mouth

because she didn't know how else to show him, tell him how much she loved him and how much she wanted to be his family.

SPENCE AUTOMATICALLY PUT his arms around Olympia as her lips sealed against his, her clever little tongue sweeping the inside of his mouth. But there was more than heat in that kiss. As she nibbled at his lips and along his jaw, he could hear her breathy voice saying, "I love you, Spence. I love that you're my family. I love that you want just me, and I love that you think you're a cowboy."

"I am a cowboy," he said to her as he buried his face into her neck, taking care to not squash their baby. "And you're a cowgirl. My cowgirl. Together we're going to breed us a passel of cowpokes."

"A passel?" she laughed.

"Why, darlin', what did you expect, since you can't keep your hands off me?" His heart filled with warmth and a deep-burning love. This was where he found happiness. Not in the courtroom. Not on the golf course, not even getting Muffin to stop biting him without a bribe. Here in Olympia's arms with their child cradled between them—

"Dad, Limpy, whatcha doin'?"

Now it was complete. Spence pulled his son into their circle, and the four of them stood in each other's arms, then Audie let out a fart, followed by Calvin imitating the sound with a gleeful giggle.

His cowgirl looked up at him, her dark eyes sparking with happiness. "So this is better than being a rodeo cowgirl?"

"Why, ma'am, yes it is. Because we all worship the

ground your boot steps on, even if you don't make the eight seconds."

"That's bull riding, cowboy. Maybe Peanut will join the rodeo."

"If she wants, but let's get her to sleep through the night first."

Spence released them and turned to his…their son. "Come on, Calvin, let's check Pasquale while the girls get cleaned up, then we need to have a family meeting."

Chapter Eighteen

"Uh-oh," Lavonda said over the phone, her voice distressed but with a hint of laughter. "Molly heard. That pony's got bat ears."

"What do you mean?" Olympia asked. She had been talking on a three-way call with Lavonda and Jessie about the upcoming ceremony, where she and Spence would renew their vows. It was supposed to be simple. Just family. And by family, her preference would have been Cal, Audie and Spence. Her two friends had other ideas of what constituted family.

"Molly heard about the wedding," Jessie clarified through the speaker.

"So?"

"So," Jessie went on patiently, "you remember what happened with Payson and me?"

"No. Absolutely not."

"Dang it, Molly," Jessie said before Olympia heard a stomp and bugle from a much larger equine.

"What's going on there?"

"Molly's got Bull all riled up, and she's trotting up and down in the barn," Jessie said, then called, "You are not going to be in this wedding. She just said they're not… Hey, don't open that." Jessie's voice was raised in alarm.

"Gotta go," Lavonda said. "We're in the midst of an all-out pony rebellion here."

"EXPLAIN TO ME again why we're doing this?" Olympia asked as Lavonda pulled at her wedding dress. It was an off-the-rack, lacy number from Dillard's that Lavonda and Jessie had insisted she wear.

"Because," Jessie said patiently, jiggling a fussy Audie, "we all love a party and felt cheated not getting to see you hog-tie Spence. Plus, Molly wanted to be in another wedding."

"Since Molly is not my pony, I'm not sure how it was my problem that she was 'upset' about not being the ring bearer again," Olympia said.

"We're family, and that pony is family," Jessie said. "What do you have to complain about? Spence negoti-ated a good deal with his brother for 'babysitting gratis and without just compensation until such time as those services are no longer needed.'"

"We were supposed to go see your brother, Danny," Olympia said. "He could have said the words again to convince Cal we were really, really married, then we were going to go out to dinner. That was it. Look at what's happened now. There's a whole yard of people, and the house is full, and—"

"But because of the wedding, you got the house up-graded," Rickie said with no sympathy. "I think this is one of them there win-wins." Her sister imitated Spence's cowboy drawl exactly.

"I'll take Peanut," Olympia said, reaching out her arms for the baby, hoping that would settle her nerves.

Why was she nervous? She and Spence were already married. Had been married for more than a year now.

"No," Lavonda and Rickie said with horror.

Wrinkling her nose, her sister added, "She'll spit up on you or leak some other bodily fluid."

Jessie said to Rickie, "You clean up horse poop, and you're worried about a baby?"

Rickie stood back and gave Olympia the thumbs-up. "Time to go, so we can get this party started before Cal runs out of gummy worms for Molly."

"What is it about this family that we can't do weddings like everyone else?" Jessie asked as she followed Olympia out of the master bedroom, which had been enlarged in the ranch renovation—paid for with a home-equity loan co-signed by Jessie and Payson. The furnishings had been added courtesy of an online gift registry Lavonda had created. Then there was a lot of free labor from friends and family to get the whole project done—well, nearly done anyway.

"We're rebels at heart?" Lavonda suggested.

"We're free spirits," Rickie said.

"No. We're bullheaded cowgirls, according to Spence," Olympia added. "Or maybe that's Muffin-headed. That horse has nearly out-stubborned me."

"I hear Spence has horses all figured out," Jessie said.

"He thought he did until he got bit when he tried to make Molly come out of Muffin's stall."

Olympia shut up when she saw they were on the patio, and everyone turned to look at her. The aisle between the rows of borrowed folding chairs was filled with family and friends. Her stomach fluttered, not with Peanut kicks, but the excitement of saying in front of everyone that she loved Spence, that she wanted to make a family with him. Olympia looked down the aisle at her husband, splendid in his finest Western suit and hat. She glanced to her right, where Cal stood with Molly's flower-decorated lead in his hand and decked out in a suit just like his dad's. Audie let out a squeal from behind her. She'd spotted her father. That baby was smitten. *Yeah, just like you, cowgirl.*

"Get a move on," Lavonda said with a light push as soon as Molly and Cal started down the aisle.

Olympia stepped toward her cowboy, followed by her friends and her baby girl. Her sisters watched her with big goofy grins. Even Mama and Grammy had come. Spence's parents sat primly, his mother's perfectly matched outfit looking out of place. Jessie said not to pay attention because the woman wore only Chanel.

Olympia caught the light scent of licorice. Her nerves settled, and her grip firmed on the small bouquet that Lavonda insisted she carry.

"You ready, darlin'?" Spence asked as he pulled her close and they faced Danny Leigh—little brother to Jessie and Lavonda. He was mayor of some town somewhere, giving him "marryin' rights for the whole danged state."

"Of course. A cowgirl never shows fear," she whispered back with a smile. "'Cause only a real cowgirl would take on you and your wild herd of kiddos."

"That's right," he whispered back. "Maybe we can see how good you are with a rope later?"

"Hey," Danny, light eyed like his sister Jessie, said. "That is stuff that I don't need to know. Are you ready?"

Olympia looked at her fake-as-a-three-dollar-bill

cowboy and only saw the real deal today. She nodded. He squeezed her hand and gave her a full-dimpled smile.

"DAD," CALVIN SAID, his sister seated at his feet on her heavily padded butt, happily patting the dirt. Spence sighed. The pretty outfit his mother had purchased for Audie was now dusty and streaked with what he hoped was cake. "Dad," Calvin said louder.

"Yeah, buddy."

"You and Limpy are married, right? We're a real family?"

"We were married before."

His son gave him the look, which basically said, "Don't give me that line, I'm scary smart, and I know it's total BS."

"There was a ring this time, right?"

"Calvin, you led Molly down the aisle with the rings on her pillow."

"I just wanted to make sure. You could have done a magic trick."

Calvin had recently become fascinated by magic. Audie scooted closer to Spence's foot and started covering his pointed cowboy boot with dirt. He couldn't help but smile down at the mess of inky hair on her head as she concentrated on his foot. That was her mother. That fierce determination.

"So." Calvin interrupted Spence's focus on his little girl. "It's real, and we both get to live here forever."

"Yup. That's why we made the house bigger—so we'd all fit." Spence thought that some logic might help Calvin. He understood that the boy might be worried about where he'd land after his early life. Spence could see Calvin was leading up to something, but he didn't know what. "You were even on the crew and put in the kitchen tile with Uncle Payson and Uncle Danny."

"Because it's easy to clean, right?"

Spence looked at Calvin carefully, hoping he could read his big brain. "That's what—"

"Hey, what are you guys doing? And why is Peanut sitting in the dirt?" Olympia asked, bending over to scoop up the little girl, obviously not worried about the drooling mouth that immediately gave her kisses or the grubby hands that yanked at her dress.

"Calvin was asking me about our flooring choices," Spence said, enjoying the sight of his wife and little girl. They both grinned at him.

"Aah," Olympia said with understanding, though what she could understand, he had no idea. "You want to make sure the floor can handle a puppy?"

"What?" Spence asked. "Calvin, we told you—"

"Aunt Jo said that the puppy needs a home bad," he answered fiercely. Apparently, Olympia's sister Jolene, who worked as a vet tech and had a menagerie at her farm, was trying to unload one of her crew.

"We've talked about this, Calvin. No dogs, and especially not a puppy. You're in school all day, I'm at work and Olympia has the horses to take care of."

"I'd take care of him, and I don't need to go to the stupid school anyway. I could go to cyberschool or you could teach me or you could ask Mimi and Grandpa Stu for money for a tutor."

Spence closed his eyes to find patience. Calvin's therapist had said the boy was excited and happy about Spence and Olympia renewing their vows. The woman had also said that Calvin needed a lot of stability and as-

surance that the adults in his life were sticking around.
She thought that his insistence on getting a puppy was
to create a connection he had more control over. Or,
Spence thought cynically, he could just be a little boy
who'd watched too many movies about how cool it was
to have a dog.

He'd taken too long to answer, and Olympia said,
"Cal, Aunt Jo is always trying to give away a dog or
a cat. You know, she helps rescue animals. It's part of
her job."

"I know, but this puppy is different."

"Really? What's his story?"

Oh, no, Olympia sounded interested, as if she was
actually considering adding a puppy to the ranch. It had
taken threats from him of taking away Xbox and computer privileges to get Petunia to the sanctuary.

"Aunt Jo said that he's deaf and that he has to have
an operation on his heart, then he'll be better. She said
that deaf dogs are special and that Max is really, really
smart. He already knows how to sit. She thinks that he
can learn sign language. I found a YouTube video, and
I've already learned how to tell him to stay, fetch, roll
over, play dead—" Calvin gulped a breath of air.

"Buddy," Spence stepped in. "We've talked about
this."

"But, Dad, he might never get adopted," Calvin said.
"He's got problems. People don't want puppies with
problems, Aunt Jo says."

Spence glared at his wife. They'd been together long
enough that he knew she had a very good idea what he
was thinking—that her sister should keep her big mouth
shut. But Olympia just smiled.

Darn. He'd lost another argument, without a word.

He knew defeat, but that didn't mean he couldn't negotiate for better terms, later, alone, in bed.

OLYMPIA SMILED AT the frowning Lavonda, who was completely baffled by the change in plans. She didn't understand that Spence and Olympia didn't want to be alone for a honeymoon. They wanted to have their family around them. Olympia guessed sometime soon she and Spence would be willing to let the children go to sleepovers, and that they'd take getaways from the ranch, but not now, not today. Not on this day when Olympia finally had settled into her new dream of a family, of loving Spence and having all of it—from a husband to children to a ranch full of strays. Later tonight, they'd celebrate by burning their prenup and its addendum in the chiminea, then they'd have their own fun under the stars. She shivered in anticipation.

"I know what you're thinking," Lavonda said, her delicate and very ladylike features scrunched into a frown. "It's X-rated, and a woman not getting any shouldn't be exposed to such blatant—"

"Uh-oh," Jessie interrupted as she walked up. "Does Limpy have 'honeymoon eyes'?"

"Honeymoon eyes?" What the heck were they talking about? Olympia wondered about these sisters some days.

Jessie grinned. "That's what she said Payson and I looked like after we got married. That sometimes we got 'honeymoon eyes,' which meant we'd kick her out so we could get busy."

Lavonda put her hands on her hips, glaring at her older and taller sister. "It was disgusting. Even Mama and Daddy commented on the goo-goo eyes."

Jessie just shrugged.

"So, are you and Spence all packed?" Jessie asked.

"No. We're staying here with the kids, and the puppy'll be here in a few days."

"Your sister broke down Spence's resistance?" Jessie asked.

"Something like that," Olympia answered. She loved the two women, but she really wanted everyone to go home now. She wanted to enjoy her family, the little unit that made her feel safe and whole.

"See what I mean?" Lavonda accused. "See her face?"

"I see what you mean, which also means it's time for everyone to hit the highway. Lucky for you, Molly has decided, now that Muffin is totally in love with her, it's time to go home," Jessie said with a smile. "Are you sure you don't want us to take the kids just for tonight? You can drive to Phoenix tomorrow and pick them up."

"No, we're good with everyone here."

Jessie stepped forward and gave Olympia a hug, whispering in her ear, "I understand. This is a great way to celebrate, and don't let Lavonda tell you any different. I hope I get to feel the same way soon."

Olympia stepped back and nodded, but she'd stopped paying attention because Spence was walking toward her with the kids.

"Oops. I see I've lost you."

Olympia turned to her friend. "It'll happen. I know it's not for lack of trying, and Payson will be coming back to Arizona permanently in a month or two. Then you'll see, you'll be pregnant in a second."

Jessie's smile didn't reach her eyes, but Olympia

didn't push. She just hugged her friend and sister-in-law.

"Payson says to shake a boot because Molly has eaten every gummy worm and has spotted the leftover cake," Spence said to Jessie, giving Olympia a questioning look. She tilted her head so that he knew they'd talk about it later.

"All right. I tried to take the munchkins, but Olympia said no. You're good with it, too?"

Spence nodded and came to stand beside Olympia. She felt whole again. She waved Jessie away. "Everyone else gone?"

"Yep," Spence said, the arm around her shoulder moving down her back to caress her rear, giving her a promise of what he was planning for their second honeymoon.

Two hours later, she and Spence sat on the patio, enjoying the warm night air and an adult beverage. They held hands like teenagers, stretching out the anticipation of what would be happening in the bedroom soon.

"I love you," Spence said.

"I love you, too…and Peanut and Cal."

"Yep. Them, too. Are you sure you're okay with staying here tonight?"

"Absolutely. We can always spend a night on our own. Today…tonight is about celebrating our family. How can we do that if we're not with the kids?" How her tune had changed. She smiled because she liked this new melody. Sheets. That was sappy.

"Come here," Spence said, his voice deep and husky. He patted his lap. She sat down and cuddled into him, inhaling deeply his licorice scent.

The kids were settled, and now it was time for the two of them to celebrate. He nuzzled her neck and cupped her breast. She shivered. She wanted this as badly as she knew he did. She squirmed against him as he lifted the hem of her wedding dress.

"You naughty woman," he breathed.

"I'm a cowgirl. I'm always ready for a good time." Olympia wanted him. Now. Instead, he kissed her gently, and the warmth of the desert air caressed her exposed skin. She pulled herself around and straddled his legs, facing him.

"Don't you want to—?" Spence tried to put words together, but her busy hands made that tough. He wanted to tell her that the bed was close by, but her cowgirl-strong thighs wrapped around him and she kissed him hard.

She knew she could fly free with him and never lose herself. Spence and his love rooted her in a world that allowed her to fearlessly explore her own joy. She knew that he'd never let her stumble and fall.

"I love you, Spencer David MacCormack, the baddest cowboy in Arizona."

Spence held her close. "I love you, my sweet-as-apple-pie cowgirl."

Then she was flying as they kissed again, totally connected as he pulled her close. Love made it all possible.

* * * * *

COMING NEXT MONTH FROM

HARLEQUIN®

American Romance®

Available September 1, 2015

#1561 LONE STAR BABY
McCabe Multiples • by Cathy Gillen Thacker
Drs. Gavin Monroe and Violet McCabe have just been named co-guardians of an orphaned baby girl. Working together to find a permanent home for the child, they may just discover that the three of them make a perfect family.

#1562 THE COWBOY AND THE LADY
Forever, Texas • by Marie Ferrarella
Once the black sheep of Forever, Texas, Jackson White Eagle now runs a ranch for troubled teens. When Deborah Kincannon brings her rebellious younger brother to his program, Jackson could be the one who needs help...resisting the beautiful nurse's charms!

#1563 THE DOCTOR'S ACCIDENTAL FAMILY
Safe Harbor Medical • by Jacqueline Diamond
Nurse Zady Moore doesn't want yet another dead-end relationship with a single dad. So when Dr. Nick Davis asks for her help with his toddler, she refuses—until her little goddaughter arrives on her doorstep and she needs Nick's help in return.

#1564 HER FAVORITE COWBOY
by Mary Leo
Wall Street big shot Gage Remington needs to rediscover his cowboy roots. What better way than attending a Western memorabilia conference in Durango, Colorado? While there, he meets Cori Parker, the down-to-earth doctor—and cowgirl—of his dreams!

YOU CAN FIND MORE INFORMATION ON UPCOMING HARLEQUIN® TITLES, FREE EXCERPTS AND MORE AT WWW.HARLEQUIN.COM.

HARCNM0815

REQUEST YOUR FREE BOOKS!
2 FREE NOVELS PLUS 2 FREE GIFTS!

HARLEQUIN®

American Romance®

LOVE, HOME & HAPPINESS

YES! Please send me 2 FREE Harlequin® American Romance® novels and my 2 FREE gifts (gifts are worth about $10). After receiving them, if I don't wish to receive any more books, I can return the shipping statement marked "cancel." If I don't cancel, I will receive 4 brand-new novels every month and be billed just $4.74 per book in the U.S. or $5.49 per book in Canada. That's a savings of at least 12% off the cover price! It's quite a bargain! Shipping and handling is just 50¢ per book in the U.S. and 75¢ per book in Canada.* I understand that accepting the 2 free books and gifts places me under no obligation to buy anything. I can always return a shipment and cancel at any time. Even if I never buy another book, the two free books and gifts are mine to keep forever.

154/354 HDN GHZZ

Name	(PLEASE PRINT)	

Address		Apt. #

City	State/Prov.	Zip/Postal Code

Signature (if under 18, a parent or guardian must sign)

Mail to the Reader Service:
IN U.S.A.: P.O. Box 1867, Buffalo, NY 14240-1867
IN CANADA: P.O. Box 609, Fort Erie, Ontario L2A 5X3

Want to try two free books from another line?
Call 1-800-873-8635 or visit www.ReaderService.com.

* Terms and prices subject to change without notice. Prices do not include applicable taxes. Sales tax applicable in N.Y. Canadian residents will be charged applicable taxes. Offer not valid in Quebec. This offer is limited to one order per household. Not valid for current subscribers to Harlequin American Romance books. All orders subject to credit approval. Credit or debit balances in a customer's account(s) may be offset by any other outstanding balance owed by or to the customer. Please allow 4 to 6 weeks for delivery. Offer available while quantities last.

Your Privacy—The Reader Service is committed to protecting your privacy. Our Privacy Policy is available online at www.ReaderService.com or upon request from the Reader Service.

We make a portion of our mailing list available to reputable third parties that offer products we believe may interest you. If you prefer that we not exchange your name with third parties, or if you wish to clarify or modify your communication preferences, please visit us at www.ReaderService.com/consumerschoice or write to us at Reader Service Preference Service, P.O. Box 9062, Buffalo, NY 14240-9062. Include your complete name and address.

HAR15

SPECIAL EXCERPT FROM

H HARLEQUIN®

American Romance®

*Doctors Gavin Monroe and Violet McCabe
have just been named co-guardians of an orphaned
baby girl and need to work together to find the child
a permanent home...*

Read on for a sneak peak of
LONE STAR BABY, *from* **Cathy Gillen Thacker**'s
McCABE MULTIPLES miniseries.

The usual idealism shining in her pretty brown eyes, Violet turned to Gavin, frowned and said, "Obviously we can't adopt baby Ava together." She walked back outside and he followed her. "We barely know each other."

Barely?

While it was true they hadn't hung out together as kids and had run in different social circles—it was certainly different now that they were both physicians.

Irked to find her so quick to discount the time they *had* spent together, Gavin stepped in once again to lend a hand unpacking the trailer, pointing out, "We've worked together for the past five years while we completed our residencies and fellowship training."

"You know what I mean. Yes, I know your preferred ways of dealing with certain medical situations, just as you surely know mine. But when it comes to the intricate personal details of your life, I don't know you any better than I know the rest of the staff at the hospital." Violet plucked a lamp base out of the pile of belongings, rooting

HAREXP0815

around until she found the shade. "And you don't really know me at all, either."

Gavin's jaw tightened. Oh, he knew her, all right. Maybe better than she thought.

For instance he knew her preferred coffee was a skinny vanilla latte. And that she loved enchiladas above all else—to the point she'd sampled all twenty-five types from the local Tex-Mex restaurant.

He tore his gaze from the barest hint of cleavage in the V of her T-shirt and concentrated instead on the dismayed hint of color sweeping her delicate cheeks.

"And whose fault is that?" he inquired.

"Mine, obviously," she said with a temperamental lift of her finely arched brow, "since I prefer to keep a firewall between my professional and private lives."

More like a nuclear shield, he thought grimly.

Don't miss
LONE STAR BABY
by Cathy Gillen Thacker,
available September 2015 everywhere
Harlequin® American Romance®
books and ebooks are sold.

www.Harlequin.com

Copyright © 2015 by Cathy Gillen Thacker

HAREXP0815

THE WORLD IS BETTER WITH

Romance

Harlequin has everything from contemporary, passionate and heartwarming to suspenseful and inspirational stories.

Whatever your mood, we have a romance just for you!

Connect with us to find your next great read, special offers and more.

 /HarlequinBooks

@HarlequinBooks

www.HarlequinBlog.com

www.Harlequin.com/Newsletters

HARLEQUIN®

A *Romance* FOR EVERY MOOD™

www.Harlequin.com

SERIESHALOAD2015